Date: 8/19/20

GRA AKATSUKI V.3
Akatsuki, Natsume,
Konosuba : the strongest
duo's turn /an explosion on

KONOSUBA:
an EXPLOSION
on WONDERFUL
WORLD!
3
STRONGEST DUO'S TURN

Megumin

My name is Megumin! Arch-wizard and wielder of the most powerful of all offensive magic, Explosion!

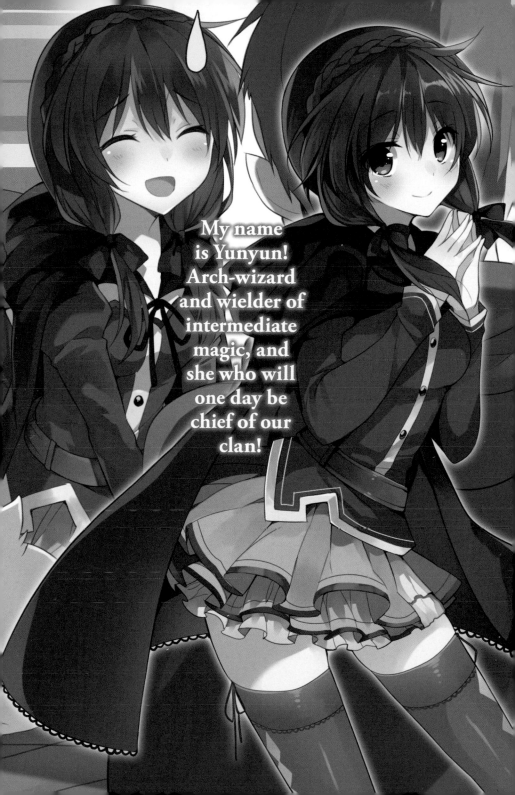

My name is Yunyun! Arch-wizard and wielder of intermediate magic, and she who will one day be chief of our clan!

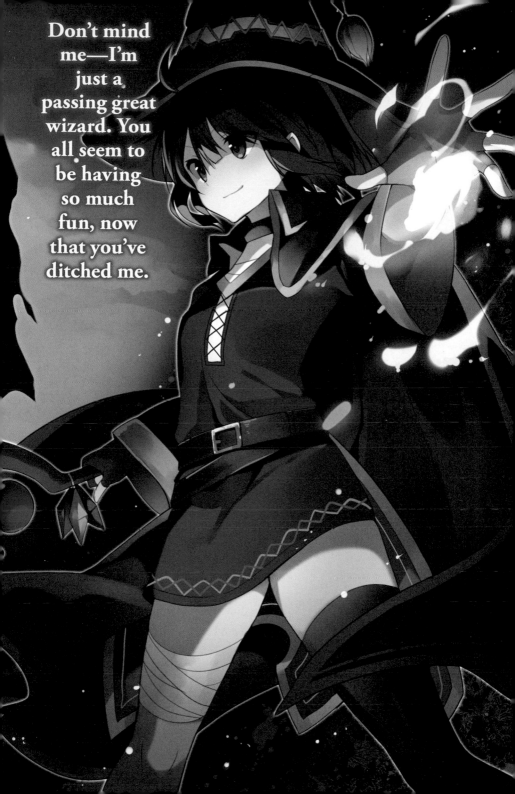

Don't mind me—I'm just a passing great wizard. You all seem to be having so much fun, now that you've ditched me.

KONOSUBA: AN EXPLOSION ON THIS WONDERFUL WORLD!

3

CONTENTS

KONOSUBA: AN EXPLOSION ON THIS WONDERFUL WORLD!

THE STRONGEST DUO!'s TURN

3

NATSUME AKATSUKI

ILLUSTRATION BY
KURONE MISHIMA

YEN
ON
NEW YORK

KONOSUBA: AN EXPLOSION ON THIS WONDERFUL WORLD!

NATSUME AKATSUKI

Translation by Kevin Steinbach
Cover art by Kurone Mishima

KONO SUBARASHI SEKAI NI SHUKUFUKU WO! SPIN OFF · KONO SUBARASHI SEKAI NI BAKUEN WO! Vol. 3
FUTARI HA SAIKYOU! NO TURN
© Natsume Akatsuki, Kurone Mishima 2015
First published in Japan in 2015 by KADOKAWA CORPORATION, Tokyo.
English translation rights arranged with KADOKAWA CORPORATION, Tokyo, through TUTTLE-MORI AGENCY, INC., Tokyo.

English translation © 2020 by Yen Press, LLC

Yen On
150 West 30th Street, 19th Floor
New York, NY 10001

Visit us at yenpress.com
facebook.com/yenpress
twitter.com/yenpress
yenpress.tumblr.com
instagram.com/yenpress

First Yen On Edition: July 2020

Yen On is an imprint of Yen Press, LLC.
The Yen On name and logo are trademarks of Yen Press, LLC.

The publisher is not responsible for websites (or their content) that are not owned by the publisher.

Library of Congress Cataloging-in-Publication Data
Names: Akatsuki, Natsume, author. | Mishima, Kurone, 1991– illustrator. | Steinbach, Kevin, translator.
Title: Konosuba, an explosion on this wonderful world! / Natsume Akatsuki ; illustration by Kurone Mishima ; cover art by Kurone Mishima.
Other titles: Kono subarashii sekai ni bakuen wo! (Light novel). English
Description: First Yen On edition. | New York, NY : Yen On, 2019.
Identifiers: LCCN 2019038569 | ISBN 9781975359607 (v. 1 ; trade paperback) | ISBN 9781975387044 (v. 3 ; trade paperback) | ISBN 9781975387020 (v. 2 ; trade paperback)
Subjects: CYAC: Fantasy. | Magic—Fiction. | Future life—Fiction.
Classification: LCC PZ7.1.A38 Km 2019 | DDC 741.5/952—dc23
LC record available at https://lccn.loc.gov/2019038569

ISBNs: 978-1-9753-8704-4 (paperback)
978-1-9753-8705-1 (ebook)

10 9 8 7 6 5 4 3 2 1

LSC-C

Printed in the United States of America

Prologue

A young man was shouting from far away. I closed my eyes and listened while I took stock of my situation.

I was in Axel, the town for novice adventurers.

Also called the "starter town," it was where low-level adventurers gathered to look for companions. That's right: I had left the village of the Crimson Magic Clan to go on a journey, and my first act had been to make my way here, accompanying a merchant caravan as a bodyguard.

And my reward for my hard work was this inn...

"I should never have come to this alternate world! I want a mulligan! I demand a do-over!"

Just as I was lost in thought, the shouting started again.

...*Alternate world?*

Someone outside must be very drunk.

"You think I *want* to do this over again, you stupid NEET?! The last thing I wanted was to be stuck with a weak good-for-nothing—give me a hero, or a handsome guy to spoil me rotten!"

"Ooh, you're in for it now, you—!"

I wondered what they could possibly be fighting about. I got out of bed and opened the window to find a warm sunset illuminating the sky over Axel. I looked down at the street, which was full of adventurers done with work for the day—they looked tired, but everyone was smiling as they strolled past.

They wore whatever equipment they could scrape together; most of them weren't even in proper armor. It was also obvious that many of the parties had unbalanced structures, lacking a proper ratio of front-row to back-row members.

But that was exactly what you would expect.

After all, this was a town full of novices. It would be my proverbial starting line, just a place I passed through on my way to bigger and better things. I hardly expected to stay long at all.

As I gazed out the window, resting my elbows on the sill, I saw one adventurer with dirty golden hair, seemingly on his way home from work, turn to the companions trailing along behind him.

"Yo, we hunted way more of 'em than we expected today! Let's go all out!"

"Aww, yeah! I'm all about that Ever-Warm Emerald Neroid-and-Gelatinous-Slime combo platter!"

"Whoo-hoo! It's a cold beer and fried frog legs for me!"

"Geez, guys, I think we should wait to spoil ourselves until we've picked up some better equipment… Eh, I guess once in a while, it can't hurt… Beer and frog legs for me, too!"

*   *   *

…I had big plans, plans to work my mojo as an Arch-wizard until the whole world knew my name. This town was never going to interest me for very long.

"Rin! Keith! Taylor! Let's drink till dawn!"

But the adventurers around here really did seem to be having fun.

Chapter 1

Outlaws of the Starter Town

1

After defeating Chomusuke's stalker, Arnes, we collected our gold (a token of gratitude) from the caravan leader, who even made arrangements for us to stay at a very nice inn.

"You gotta be kidding! A coddled child of the modern world, sleeping in a stable?! There's no way!"

I *had* been sleeping ever since I got to this town and was awakened by a shout from downstairs.

Our dear caravan leader had gotten us a room on the far end of the second floor.

There was another cry, one that carried all the way to my new abode.

"I don't want to sleep with the horses any more than you do! But we don't have any *money*, which means we don't have any *choice*!"

The commotion seemed to be coming from someone—or a couple of people—who couldn't stand the thought of sleeping in the stables. Some novice adventurers who had just gotten into town, perhaps. "This is so not what I imagined being an adventurer would be like! Adventurers are supposed to make scads of money, stay in the best rooms, and drink until they can't see the next day!"

"And telling me that accomplishes what? Nothing! We only have a thousand eris left from the money that old Eris follower gave us, okay? We'll use it to get some dinner, and then we're going to sleep!"

"Damn it all! I didn't come here to live like this!"

With the argument still ringing in my ears, I went to visit Yunyun next door.

Axel, the town where beginning adventurers gathered. If you were an adventurer, this was where you got your start.

"Yunyun, are you up? I am, thanks to some noisy adventurers. Want to go eat something downstairs?"

When I knocked on the door, I was greeted by Yunyun, who looked sleepy.

"You didn't have to force yourself to get up if you were still asleep."

"…No, I'll go. I'm so rarely invited out to eat."

. . . .

That tugged at my heartstrings, but anyway, I led Yunyun downstairs.

Most inns were set up the same way: rooms up top, cafeteria and tavern down below. We must have come during peak hours, because the tavern was a zoo as we found our seats and ordered the fried-frog platter, apparently Axel's signature dish. As we devoured our meals, Yunyun and I consulted about what to do next.

"All right. I know we have only just arrived after many travails, but when you find yourself in an unknown city, you cannot rest on your laurels. We must decide what we're going to do tomorrow and thereafter."

"Right. I think for starters, we have to begin taking quests to support ourselves. And that means finding companions."

Finding companions. That suggested a visit to the town's Adventurers Guild was in order.

"Is that what you intend to do, Yunyun? Using Explosion consumes all my MP and leaves me immobilized, so *I'll* need someone who can attend to me, but I think *you* should be able to accomplish a simple quest even solo."

"I don't know. I get so nervous when I'm by myself and surrounded by monsters—and I actually *want* some friends to adventure with. Staying in the same inn together, sharing meals. Toasting one another at the end of a big quest... Huh. I left the village in such a rush, I didn't really think about it, but this is starting to sound pretty nice..." Yunyun speared bits of fried frog with her fork and mumbled to herself.

"I suppose that settles what we will do tomorrow, then. I hear there is a bulletin board at the Adventurers Guild for those looking for party members. We should give it a go. It would also be a good opportunity to ask how to go about undertaking quests."

I left Yunyun to her starry-eyed fantasies and decided to press the diners around me for information.

After all, I had another reason for coming to this town.

"Pardon me, but may I ask you a few questions?"

"'Course, li'l lady—whatcha need? What brings you to a place like this at a time like now?"

"Yeah, your mommy's gonna be worried about you, kid. Better run on home."

I attempted to interrogate two older men at a nearby table but found myself being treated like a suckling babe.

"I know I may not be the most physically impressive, but I *am* an adventurer. Look at this!" Annoyed by their condescension, I flashed my Adventurer's Card at them.

"G-gosh, gee, sorry about that! So what can I do ya fer?"

"As I said, I just need to ask you a few questions. I've been told there's a mage in this town who can use Explosion. Do you know anything about that?"

""Explosion?"" Both men looked perplexed. Didn't they know the name of a spell when they heard one?

"It is the ultimate offensive magic. I came to this town based on reports that there was a beautiful, large-chested wizard here who could use it…"

"'Beautiful' and 'large-chested,' eh…? Aww, hey, I think she means the shopkeeper!"

"The penniless proprietor! Yeah, sounds like her!"

""The penniless proprietor'?" This was not the response I had expected.

"She runs a shop full of magical items—locally famous place."

"A great wizard, used to be an adventurer herself."

A former adventurer and great wizard? Could she really be the one I was searching for? This "penniless proprietor" business bothered me, though. The woman I'd met had seemed so collected and capable. But maybe that didn't mean she was a decent businesswoman?

I asked them where this shop was and committed the location to memory. I could go find the woman anytime. But when I did, I wanted her to see how amazing I had grown up to be…

"…Maybe I'll wait until I have become a proper, self-sufficient adventurer."

The chance to finally meet her was within my grasp, but I found myself with a case of cold feet.

2

"Come now, Yunyun—let us go! Let us seize the day!"

"F-fine, okay, I'm coming, but I don't understand how you can be so fired up first thing in the morning."

Having finished our basic survey of the town, it was time to go off to the Guild.

"I do not understand how you *cannot* be. Today is the day, the moment our illustrious and long-awaited careers as adventurers begin! The pulse-pounding battles with powerful enemies yet unknown! The monsters who will be blown away by my Explosion! I'm practically bursting just thinking about them! Of course I am fired up!" I violently waved my staff with excitement as we made our way through town.

"Okay, okay! I get it—just keep your voice down!" Yunyun said, glancing around as if she was embarrassed.

It was still too early for many people to be out on the streets. We arrived at the Adventurers Guild first thing in the morning to look for companions.

On the other side of this door waited a gathering of would-be heroes. I stood before the entrance, breathing roughly out of my nostrils as I turned to Yunyun.

"Are you ready? At a time like this, the first impression can make or break you. This is the Adventurers Guild, a wretched hive of scum and villainy—I'm certain they will have nothing but ridicule for two young, untried questers such as ourselves. When we open this door, we must proclaim ourselves with the utmost authority and drama! We cannot let them mock the Crimson Magic Clan!"

"What?! W-we do?! W-we can't! Let's not—we'll only draw attention to ourselves!"

"That is exactly the point! Sometimes I cannot fathom you, Yunyun! Come now. Let us go in!"

"Ohhhh… Please don't let us get mixed up with anyone scary; please don't let us get mixed up with anyone scary…"

As I opened the door, I flung back my cape!

"My name is Megumin! Greatest genius of the Crimson Magic Clan and wielder…of…"

There was no one inside.

"O-oh God, I'm so embarrassed…!!" Behind me, Yunyun held Chomusuke in her arms; she was beet red, and her shoulders were shaking. I felt my own face get a little bit hot.

"Yes, I'm coming… Goodness, what brings you here so early?"

So there wasn't quite *no one* inside—a woman, older than us, appeared from another room. Probably a staff member.

When I took a fresh look around, I discovered that not only were there no adventurers looking for work, but even the attached tavern was bereft of customers. I collected myself and went over to the woman, who had taken a seat at the counter.

"H-hello. I'm Megumin, an Arch-wizard. I'm, *ahem*, new to the adventuring business, so I'm not quite sure what to do…"

"Oh my, those eyes. You're from the Crimson Magic Clan, aren't you? I do seem to recall the Clan creates Adventurer's Cards for everyone when they reach school age. So you already have a card, right? I'll need to check it before you start adventuring, just to make sure you don't have any criminal history or anything…"

I was about to let the receptionist do just that when a thought occurred to me. "I'm sorry, but perhaps we could defer the card check a little while? Specifically, I'd like to wait until there are more adventurers here."

The woman gave me a quizzical look. "That's fine, I guess…"

I stepped away from the desk and sat at a nearby table.

"Megumin, aren't you going to have her look at your card? Are you sure you want me to go first?"

"Fine by me. I wish to wait until there are more people here."

Yunyun looked dubious, but she handed her card to the receptionist.

"Thank you. I'll just have a look at— Oh! It's just like you hear about the Crimson Magic Clan— Incredible! I've never seen someone with so much MP!"

"Th-thank you..."

I just sat there listening to them with a little smile on my face and waited for more people to arrive.

3

Other people slowly began filtering into the Guild until the place was alive with bar patrons. They were mainly adventurers looking for choice assignments and making plans for the day. I listened to the hum from the tavern and whispered to myself, "...Looks like it's time."

I stood up, earning a look from Yunyun, who was sitting across from me at the table, eating a plate of pasta.

"Why did you want to wait so long to have your card checked? You would've gotten through a lot quicker a few minutes ago, when there was nobody in line..."

I told Yunyun (who understood nothing) that I would be right back, then worked my way toward the crowd of people around the front desk.

There were, incidentally, unspoken rules for how one chose a receptionist at a moment like this. First preference went to the most beautiful receptionist lady. Such women were often important people of the Guild. Other times, they had surprising backstories. For example, they may have once been highly accomplished adventurers themselves. That was just common sense in this industry—or so we'd been taught in school anyway.

"All right, next please... Oh, you're the Crimson Magic Clan member from earlier, aren't you?" the receptionist (with wavy hair and a huge rack) remarked when she saw my eyes.

"As you say, ma'am. I am from the Crimson Magic Clan. Starting today, I intend to make this town my base of operations, so I've come to request that you check my Adventurer's Card."

"I see. Here, let me have a look... O-oh my goodness! This is incredible—I know they say Crimson Magic Clansfolk have tremendous Intelligence and Magic, but these numbers are amazing...!"

The receptionist's astonishment set off a buzz among the gathered adventurers. Yes! This was what I wanted. I wanted everyone to see the receptionist's surprise at my stats and start talking about me! Now no one would mock or ridicule—

"Well, not quite as amazing as that woman yesterday, but still, a very high Magic stat... Good, I see you don't have any criminal history, and your card is authentic. You may accept your first assignment whenever you're ready."

...*Huh?*

"Just a moment, please—what woman from yesterday? Are you suggesting there was someone with a higher Magic stat than mine?"

"Oh, I was referring to someone who registered as an adventurer yesterday... Her Intelligence score was too low to permit her to be a Wizard of any sort... I believe she settled on being an Arch-priest."

Arch-priest?

"Ohhh, *her*."

"*Her*."

"She was a looker, too. Damn shame... And she kept jabbering about being a goddess or something."

"If only she wasn't Axis. Oh, and if only she wasn't so bent on making a fool of herself. I would totally ask her to be in my party…"

"I'm sure she says those stupid things *because* she's an Axis priest."

The receptionist's comment had inspired a lengthy chorus of whispers from the eavesdropping adventurers.

So who was she? It must have been the Arch-priest in question, but why the contemptuous tone? In any event, if she had gone into the clergy, then she would be no obstacle to my own quest to become the strongest Arch-wizard, so it didn't much matter to me.

I had something more important to do…

"H-hey! Are you available right now? Have you decided who you're going to adventure with yet?"

"Hey, no fair! I saw her first!"

"My party has two advanced classes in it! How about it?!"

My conversation with the receptionist had inspired a frenzied contest to recruit me.

4

I was in a corner of the tavern, where a young girl and guy were introducing themselves to me.

"My name's Ryze. I'm a Warrior. And this is Laina, the Thief. Nice to meetcha!"

"My name is Megumin. A pleasure."

""…Is that your real name?""

"Yes, it is. If you have a problem with my name, I shall hear it."

"U-uh-uh! No problem! Oh yeah, I guess we did hear you were from the Crimson Magic Clan…"

"Y-yeah, I think it's a great name!"

The two of them were eager to prevent any potential rift.

I had decided to join up with this brother-sister duo. A normal adventuring party had anywhere between four and six people in it, but fewer people meant a bigger share of the loot for each member. At the moment, the only money I had to my name was the honorarium provided by the caravan leader, so I needed to start earning, and fast.

It occurred to me to glance over to the table where I had been sitting with Yunyun. She was sitting still as a stone and peering uneasily around the building. It seemed she didn't even have it in her to go through the seeking-group flyers and ask someone to let her join them. Her whispered "Excuse me..." and discreet waves of her hand were quickly lost in the bustling Guild.

This would be an excellent chance for her to work on overcoming her shyness. It would be best for me not to help and instead let her handle things on her own.

"What's up? Some other adventurer you're curious about?"

"With you joining us, Megumin, we've still only got three people in our party. There's room for someone else if you like."

"No, it's quite all right. Shall we begin with a simple hunting quest? An easy assignment will help us see how this party jibes. Call it a probationary period."

Ryze and Laina didn't object. In the distance, Yunyun, after a fair amount of dithering, had gotten some paper from the receptionist and was writing something. It seemed she had already given up on talking to anyone and decided to make her own flyer instead.

"Here's a Chestnut Rat hunt. What do you think, Megumin?"

"The Chestnut Rats should be nice and fat this time of year," Laina said. "It'll make them tasty."

I didn't know what a Chestnut Rat was. From Laina's remarks about fat and tastiness, I thought perhaps they were some kind of edible monster. This was, after all, autumn: the season of the raging appetite.

And the time when chestnuts were at their tastiest. The name of this monster was enough to make me excited.

"Well, let's do it, then!" I nodded at them, feeling a rush of excitement for my very first quest.

5

Chestnut Rats.

They were called that, I discovered, because they liked to feed on chestnuts, which made their meat soft and flavorful. About the size of a medium-ish dog, the nimble rodents would invade local farms and tear through the fall produce.

"Megumin, Megumin! There's a whole bunch of them heading in our direction! Here they come—argh, they're coming! Take them out with your magic! Laina, cover Megumin to make sure the rats don't get near her!"

"Watch out, Ryze! There's one in the shadows!"

"Yikes! Gotta be careful…!"

There was a hollow *thump* from Ryze's shield as the Chestnut Rat slammed against it.

"Leave it to me—I can wipe out a horde this size in one blow! Just buy me a little time!"

"A-are you sure?! We're not just talking about a few rodents here! O-okay, do what you need to do!"

"Ryze, keep your eyes to the front!" Laina shouted, tossing a throwing knife into the swarm of rats; her brother quickly brought up his shield. There was another thump and an unpleasant scraping sound as a Chestnut Rat's quills scratched across the metal surface. Anything less than metal equipment and the target of one of those body slams would be in a good deal of trouble.

Laina flung knife after knife, skewering individual rats, Ryze barely keeping them at bay. I felt a bead of sweat run down my cheek—maybe I was nervous, faced with the reality that failure was not an option. At last, though, my incantation was complete, and I held my staff high and shouted.

"Both of you, get some distance from the enemy! I'm going to drop it right in the middle of the swarm!"

""On it!""

They both disengaged from the rats. At almost the same instant, I unleashed my spell!

"Explooosion!"

A flash of light erupted from the end of my staff, piercing to the heart of the horde. There was a white flash as it landed and then a great, expanding heat powered by tremendous magical energy. The roar filled the entire farm as my spell annihilated the Chestnut Rats.

But the power of my explosion didn't stop there: It even consumed the chestnut trees the rats had been using as food and flung Ryze and Laina to the ground. The two of them cried out, and even I was blown back by the shock wave, but I was drunk on the satisfaction of having destroyed a huge host of monsters in one fell swoop.

…Next time, though, I would definitely have to be more aware of the area of effect of my own magic.

"*Hff… Hff…* Wh-wh-wh-wha…?"

"Wh-what in the heck was that?!"

Laina and Ryze exclaimed, surveying the devastation as they got to their feet.

"Heh! You see what becomes of Chestnut Rats who dare to stand against me! That spell was my secret technique, the ultimate magic: Explosion!"

"E-Explosion?! The same Explosion that's supposed to use so much MP that almost no one can cast it?! I've always heard it was just a gimmick, but what was gimmicky about that?! You altered the entire terrain!"

"All those rats in just one shot... I-incredible...!"

The two of them proved suitably impressed.

Then Ryze said, "Let's hit some of the other places that are having trouble with Chestnut Rats. Maybe you could use a different spell next time, though? Chestnut Rats don't usually have a big bounty on them. The way you make money is by selling their meat."

"That's true, not to mention that you decimated this entire chestnut farm. Wonder how much compensation they'll want... Ah well. Give it a hundred rats or so, and we should be back in the black. Hey..." Laina crouched down next to me.

"How long do you plan to lie there? Did you get hurt when the blast knocked you over?"

She looked so genuinely concerned.

"No, I am simply paralyzed for lack of MP. I don't believe I will be casting any more spells today..."

Chomusuke had toddled over to my prone form and was sniffing my face. Glancing at the cat, Ryze said, "Does it really take that much magic? Okay, well, let's say no explosions for a while, starting tomorrow. Just use something else. Save them for, y'know, emergencies or whatever."

"Good thinking—intermediate or advanced magic should be plenty..."

Finally, I told the talkative pair, "I can't."

"Huh...? What do you mean, you can't? Can't what?"

"Ohhh, you mean you can't use advanced magic? Like I said, I think intermediate magic should be fine..."

"No, I cannot use anything but Explosion. It is the only spell I know."

""............""

The two of them fell silent for a moment until Ryze said, "Uh, the only one? Really?"

"That's correct."

"...So it's the only spell you can use, and you can only use it once a day?"

"Yes."

They spent another moment in silence.

"".........Hang tight, Megumin. Sibling huddle.""

"Huh?"

They scurried away from me where I lay on the ground. Trapped on my back, I couldn't hear what they were saying.

After a few minutes, they came back.

"...Okay, so, uh, we've been thinking, and we feel as if maybe newbie adventurers like us can't give you the best opportunity to use your skills, Megumin."

"Y-yeah, that's right. Explosion is a better spell than we deserve. It's wasted on our party."

They didn't sound very convincing.

"Oh, that does not matter to me. You will grow into it over time..."

I thought the whole point of a party was to cover for one another's weaknesses. But Ryze promptly shook his head.

"No, no, listen, it was conceited of us—a couple of newcomers—trying to recruit an Arch-wizard of the Crimson Magic Clan!"

"Yeah, uh-huh! I m-mean, look at us—we aren't even advanced classes or anything! Think about, uh, the composition or…balance, you know?"

Hrm… If they were so insistent, then so be it.

"Paying for those chestnut trees is going to put us into debt for a while, but don't worry, we'll take care of it!"

"He's right! Someday when we're stronger, Megumin, maybe we'll be a better match for you! Let's do this again then, okay?!"

I leaned on their shoulders, as they tried to talk their way out of forming a party with me, all the way back to the Guild.

6

Well, this was a problem.

I was naturally uncomfortable making people I had just met that day pay for trees *I* had destroyed, so I went ahead and paid for the damage myself, but…

"Now I'm all out of money…"

I rested against the table, woozy with lack of magic, staring at my now very light wallet.

At a table in the corner of the tavern, quite some distance from me, Yunyun was dispiritedly picking at some food. Had no one responded to her flyer?

When I had regained enough MP that I could move a little again, curiosity got the better of me, and I went to look at what Yunyun had posted. It wasn't hard to tell which one was hers…

PARTY MEMBERS WANTED: Ideal candidates will be kind, willing to listen (even to boring stuff), won't laugh at a strange

name, will be willing to hang out even on days when there's no quest. Seeking frontline adventurer. Hopefully one of similar age. I am an Arch-wizard who has just turned thirteen.

Was she looking for party members or friends—or a boyfriend? I couldn't help thinking no one was going to respond to such an honest post…

I had an urge to go over and launch a few quips at her, but I had my hands full thinking about myself… As much as I hated to contemplate it, it seemed I had been kicked out of the team I had just joined today.

Yes, they had been very polite, claiming that it was all about *their* powers—and not mine—that was the problem, but it was really just a delicate way of booting me out…

Just when I was feeling my most depressed—

"Listen, newbie! You don't know what saury are? What rock have you been living under?!"

"Oh, I know what saury are. I know they're fish. And you want me to make this Salted Saury combo plate, right?"

The boss of the Guild tavern was berating a young man with brown hair. It was the boy I had spotted out the window of the carriage the day I arrived in Axel. I remembered him because his clothes had been so strange. I guess he had gotten himself a part-time job at the tavern. I hadn't seen him this morning—maybe today was his first day.

"That's right, saury. Fish. Scales, practically jumping out of the net. Fat and delicious this time of year."

"Yeah, I know it. Okay, I'm sorry—maybe you could repeat your instructions one more time?"

"I said go to the field around back and fetch me two saury."

"Now you're just making things up!" the young man said, flinging his apron at the boss.

Was he one of those modern, spoiled children you always hear about? What in the world was so infuriating about having to go get some saury from the field?

While the young man was fighting with his boss, a blue-haired waitress walked by, carrying a ridiculous number of ale tankards. I seemed to remember her as the young man's companion. I wondered if she had started just today, too.

"Thank you for waiting! I've got your ice-cold Crimson Neroid right here!"

"Ooh, I can't wait for— Ugh! The hell is this? This is just water! What is this, some kind of joke?"

The boss paused in his argument with the boy long enough to yell at the young woman.

"New girl! What's the big idea? You've only served the guests water all day! Where does my homemade wine keep disappearing to? You're not just drinking it all yourself, are you?!"

"N-no, I swear I'm not! I just accidentally dipped a finger in the wine…! Please listen to me! This is who I am! I'm really the goddess of water…!"

"Hey, Gramps! Hear me out! Don't think you can pull one over on us just because we're new in town! After all the time I've spent shut up in my room, I finally decide to get a damn job, and look what happens! What are you, on a power trip? You enjoy watching me try to figure out your nonsense instructions?"

The girl was about to cry, and the guy was about to explode. As for the shop owner, I could see a vein bulging on his forehead.

"Shut up, both of you! You're the ones who don't make any sense! You're both fired!"

And that was the end of their employment—the young man, whose argument was finally over, and the young woman, wailing so loudly that people were looking at her.

…Well, at least I was doing better than they were. Feeling a little of my self-confidence return, I decided to head back to the inn for today.

Yunyun and I were walking back to our accommodations.

"How did it go today, Megumin? Did you find a good party?"

"Er, not quite. We went on a quest together, but…they concluded that my powers would be wasted on them and declined to continue our working relationship."

"Oh. Yeah, your magic is so powerful, but you have to be careful when you use it." As she talked, Yunyun glanced furtively around— maybe she was curious about our new town.

"And what about you, Yunyun? I believe you made a post saying you were looking for party members. Anyone bite?"

"Yes, one person. Well, this person… I have to say, he looked like he was at least my dad's age, and when he introduced himself, he said, *'You're thirteen? 'Sup? That's what the kids say, right? I should know, because I'm obviously thirteen, too! You're looking for someone to fight on the front line, right? Just leave it to me—I'm a high-level Crusader! I'll keep you so safe!'*"

"And you turned him down, right? Please tell me you turned him down!"

"W-well, eventually, sure… But he took me to lunch, and listened to me talk, and seemed like a really nice guy. He said we should talk again tomorrow…"

"If he does try to talk to you tomorrow, you are not to respond to him under any circumstances! And you need to make a more serious seeking-group flyer!"

"Huh?! B-but it *was* serious…"

7

The next day.

When we arrived at the Guild, we were greeted by one of the waitresses.

"Good morning. Oh, you're adventurers, right? The Guild's issued a special notice, so you should go get the details from Reception."

A special notice? Curious, I wandered over to the reception area, where, lucky for me, one of the Guild employees was just in the middle of explaining what was going on.

"There have been eyewitness reports of a demon-type monster in the woods. The reports suggest that this is not just a gremlin or some other low-level monster. Demon types are frequently strong enemies, often highly intelligent and capable of using magic. The Guild is investigating the matter, but until we find out exactly what's going on, we recommend less powerful parties avoid the woods."

I heard a few sighs from the gathered adventurers. A lot of the most profitable quests took place in the woods. The standard routine for a new adventurer, I was given to understand, was to hunt Giant Toads to raise their level and then, when they could comfortably do that, to go into the woods.

Now that I knew what the special notice was about, I went over to the seeking-group board. When the caravan leader got us set up at our inn, he had paid in advance for two weeks' stay. I had to find some party members and secure a source of income before I was chased out at the end of those two weeks.

"I think I had better proactively approach somebody today," I murmured, glancing at the posts on the board. One appeared to be Yunyun's newest effort:

SEEKING PARTY MEMBERS

WANTED:
Okay if conversation suddenly stops.
Won't freak out if I visit every day.
Won't get upset if I clam up when our eyes meet.

Any class/age okay.

I guess she had decided to compromise on the class and age in hopes of attracting more responses. Although that wasn't really what I had had in mind when I told her to rewrite her post...

Without meaning to, I looked over toward the corner of the tavern where, once again, Yunyun was waiting expectantly at a table. She had set up the board game she'd brought along on our trip, playing against herself. It was the picture of pitiful, and I very nearly went to talk to her, but then I reminded myself that this was itself part of Yunyun's training.

I resumed reviewing the posts on the bulletin board. I found, for example:

SEEKING WIZARD AND PRIEST
Current members:
Sword Master
Lancer
Thief
Committed to defeating the Demon King. Interested novices also welcome.
Join us and save the world!

These people clearly had some sort of hero in mind.

WANTED: PARTY MEMBERS
We're a Crusader and a Thief.

~~We're looking for trash human beings with truly brutal fetishes.~~ One frontline and two rearguard party members. Seeking sensible, serious people!

Part of this post had obviously been scratched out. The handwriting appeared to be by two different people—and what the heck was the scratched-out part about?

Somewhere between the dreck and the crazies, I found one that looked promising.

SEEKING PARTY MEMBERS

Currently have four people in party:

Two frontline: One Eris Priest and one Archer

Wanted: Wizard

It sounded like a pretty good composition. I went to talk to the adventurers in question.

"I see. Megumin, is it? That's a very Crimson Magic–esque name. I'm Ein, the leader of this party. Here's hoping we work well together."

The man I was talking to had a sword at his hip and looked every bit the warrior. There was another person with a spear, a priest with an Eris-faith pendant around his neck, and finally someone with a huge bow on his back. They looked at me appraisingly.

They were all men, with an average level of 12. Just on the cusp of no longer being novices.

"Thank you. I hope so, too. How about we go ahead and take a quest, then, to get a feel for each other?"

"Good plan… Let's hit the woods. That would be my suggestion. I'm sure you've all heard about the demon-type monster that's supposed to be in there, but with a Crimson Magic Clan member along, I don't expect any problems. Sound good?"

"Sounds great. I can stop any demon in one hit."

The rest of the party smiled to hear me so confident.

8

Ein's shout echoed through the woods.

"There are too many of 'em! Jack, Thomas, fall back with Megumin! Rod, you're with me—we'll kick these things' butts!"

We had chosen a quest involving hunting the slimes that had been proliferating in the woods lately. This monster, the slime, was small and not very powerful, but if it managed to get enough food and grow larger, it could become an enemy so strong, even the best adventurers might find they had their hands full with it. Slimes also had a high resistance to physical attacks, and if you didn't destroy the so-called core at the center of their bodies, they would continually regrow and keep coming after you.

"Ein, our weapons hardly work on these things! Megumin, can't you use your magic?!" the man named Rod complained as he jabbed a nearby slime with his spear.

"I'm sorry, but right now, I'm afraid it isn't technically feasible; I'd catch all of you up in the spell. Maybe if we could get into a more open area…!"

"O-okay, no choice! Rod, let's do it!"

"Oh, for the love of—! All right, let's go!"

All I could do was watch from my place as the rearguard while our two fighters plunged in among the slimes.

At last they came back, breathing heavily, covered in wounds that resembled burns. Thomas, our priest, rushed over and healed them.

"We're just lucky those slimes were still small. What do you think, Megumin? Is Rod's and my fighting power everything you'd expect?"

"Yes, that was excellent. Both of you looked very cool. Next, let me show you *my* power."

Ein and Rod both blushed a little at my compliment, then turned away, saying they were looking forward to seeing what I could do.

"What the hell are Bloody Squirrels doing here?! I thought they were supposed to live deeper in the forest!"

"They're *flying* squirrels, and our attacks can't reach them! Jack, Megumin! Use your bow and your magic and shoot them out of the sky!"

As we proceeded deeper into the woods, we were beset by a swarm of Bloody Squirrels, actually a variety of flying squirrel. Ein and Rod used their weapons to keep the creatures at bay.

"I-I'm sorry, but with the squirrels clustered directly above us, I'm afraid we'd be caught up in the spell!"

"You've got to be kidding! Fine, use something less powerful… Shit, Jack! Handle this!"

"Y-yeah, sure, I'm on it!"

As Jack started dropping the squirrels out of the air, I held Chomusuke close so she wouldn't get carried off and kept my head down, just trying to stay out of everyone's way.

That was when I felt something wet land, *bloop*, right on my hat.

What could that be? The sky was so clear, it couldn't be rain…

That was when I heard Ein, holding his shield over his head, shout, "Bloody Squirrels pee on their enemies to mark them! Be careful—if it gets on you, the smell won't come off for a week!"

I jabbed my staff at the squirrel, wishing I could knock it down, but the squirrel and I both knew perfectly well that I would never reach it.

"What're you doing, Megumin?! Head down, head down!"

"Please do not try to stop me. I will not rest until I have annihilated these stupid squirrels!"

Thomas tried to hold me back, and at length Jack had taken out enough of the monsters that the rest, seeing that numbers were against them, ran away.

"I can't believe this happened to my precious hat... I guess I'll have to leave it at the inn until the stink comes out..."

We decided to take a rest after defeating the squirrels, and I spent most of my time looking ruefully at my hat, which reeked of squirrel pee. Rod came up to me where I was sitting on a tree stump.

"Hey, so. I wanted to ask you—when *can* you use your magic, exactly?"

"Wh-when...? Well, in a wide-open space where there is nothing that might unintentionally get caught up in the spell, when we are at a safe distance from our enemy—something like that, I suppose?"

After two battles where I had proven to be no help at all, Rod was rightly skeptical of my abilities.

"Huh," Ein said from beside me, standing up. "That was our bad, then, going into the forest. Let's just say that today was our turn to show off what we can do. Tomorrow, we'll hunt something on the plains."

I felt a little guilty—and, honestly, a little pathetic.

That was when it happened. There was a rustling from the underbrush, and something creeped out.

"A slime? It must have been attracted by the smell of squirrel blood. Perfect, just what we need to finish...our...quest..."

A slime had indeed appeared. But...!

"""""It's huge!"""""

This slime was the size of a shed.

"This is bad news! We can't handle one this big! Everybody run!"

"B-but we can't just leave one this size, can we?! If we don't take care of it now, it's going to be too big for *anyone* to handle soon! And with all those squirrel corpses around, it'll have all the food it wants...!"

Ein and Rod tried to decide what to do, while Jack and Thomas could only stand dumbfounded.

That was when I broke in.

"Get away from the slime."

They turned to look at me.

"Wh-what, you're going to try your magic?"

"I think we should run…"

Despite their objections, all four of them found a safe distance from the slime. It hardly seemed to notice us, perhaps because there was more convenient food lying around in great abundance. My party members crept back behind me as I began to incant my magic. I heard Rod and Ein whispering behind me.

"H-hey, aren't slimes supposed to have strong magic defense? The little guys are one thing, but I don't think even a Crimson Magic Clan member can take on something that size!"

"Shhh, keep it to yourself. This is the perfect chance to see what our new recruit can do. She doesn't have to kill it—if she can even damage a slime that big, she's more than welcome as a member of our party."

Then came Jack, already edging away: "Let's give up on the reward this time. A slime that big, we have to get back to the Guild and let them know right away!"

"I'll bet we'd get a reward just for telling them about one that big…… Huh? H-hey, what spell is that?!" Thomas the priest said, shocked, as he caught a few words of my incantation.

"What's up, Thomas? Something going on with the newbie's magic?"

"Ooh, there's electricity gathering all around Megumin. Is it some kind of lightning spell?"

Ein and Rod sounded a lot more interested than Thomas did.

Thomas, the one other person in this party who could use magic, had grasped that the spell that was about to be unleashed would be on an extraordinary scale. When the others saw how pale he had gotten, they took a fresh look at me.

"H-hey, Megumin. We're not saying you have to take out that slime or whatever, all right? There isn't an adventurer in this town who could do in one that size. If we let the Guild know, they'll call somebody from another town, someone stronger."

"Y-yeah, are you okay? I feel this…vibration in the air…"

Ein and Rod didn't sound quite as confident anymore. I just kept chanting, pointing my staff at the slime, which was going to town on the dead squirrels.

"J-just a second—I think we could be in a lot of trouble here! We need to get farther away, a *lot* farther!"

"Huh? What are you babbling about, Thomas? We're already far away. Nothing she's about to use could possibly—"

That was as far as Rod got before I finished my incantation.

"Get your heads down, please, everyone! No slime is a match for my secret magic!"

The four adventurers threw themselves to the ground.

"*Explooosion*!!"

Light flew from my staff, piercing the slime's body. The huge form swelled up, and with a blinding flash, there came a blast wind powerful enough to knock down the nearby trees. The roar sent every bird in the area scuttling into the sky, and the shock wave shook the branches of every tree that hadn't been knocked over.

When the smoke cleared, the slime was gone, leaving only me, all out of magic, and the other four, likewise on the ground.

…Next time, I would have to make sure to have even more distance.

9

Back at the Guild tavern. I was slumped on the table, bereft of MP, while Ein and the others celebrated around me, draining mug after mug of beer, as they had been doing all afternoon.

"Hoooly moly, that's the Crimson Magic Clan for you—what a punch!"

"I've never seen anything like it! The sheer destruction that spell left behind was enough to have me shaking in my boots!"

"Magic isn't even supposed to work on slimes—and she defeated it in one hit..."

The three of them showered me with praise.

Then there was Rod, sitting there with a glass of juice in his hand. "Er, *ahem*. Guess I owe you an apology. I was starting to think you were bluffing, just pretending to know magic." He held out the juice with a bow, and I looked up and shook my own head.

"Please do not apologize to me yet, for there is something that I, too, must say."

The four of them looked at one another doubtfully.

"The truth is, Explosion, which you witnessed earlier, is the only spell I can use. And I can only use it once per day. I am confident it can overcome any opponent, no matter how strong, but does this party expect to tangle with creatures like that on a daily basis?"

Ein gulped audibly. "...You don't know any other spells? Like intermediate magic or something?"

"I'm afraid not."

"...Hey, it's fine if you can't use it right now—we'll help you raise your level, and you can learn intermediate magic when you're good and ready..."

"I don't intend to learn anything that doesn't contribute directly to the power of my Explosion."

"""""   """""
......

The promptness of my answer caused them to fall silent.

"L-listen. All of us in this party, we figure it's good enough to get by earning our keep on small monsters. We don't really have any plans to hunt big game. I'm real sorry, but maybe you could try another group...?"

I took my reward for the day and said my good-byes to the four men, then dragged my MP-less self away, thinking about the matter fretfully.

Was it possible I wasn't a genius after all? Was it possible no one anywhere needed me?

...No, it was too soon to be getting bent out of shape. I had been in this town for only three days.

As I sipped the juice Rod had given me, I suddenly noticed that Yunyun—who was supposedly looking for a party just like I was—was sitting in exactly the same place she had been that morning, still playing her game by herself.

I went over and gave her a firm slap on the shoulder from behind.

"E-eep?! Hello nice to meet you my name is Yunyun I'm an Arch-wizard but I can still only use intermediate—"

She jumped up and spun around, spewing some kind of rehearsed introduction, but her face fell as she saw me standing there.

"What a reaction! Here I take pity on you sitting by yourself in a corner like the loneliest girl in the world, and this is the thanks I get!"

"'The loneliest girl in the world'? Don't call me that! It's still only been two days since I put that bulletin up; I'm sure someone will come!"

…I didn't think I had even seen anyone look at her flyer.

I sat down across from Yunyun and started lining up the game pieces.

"Hey, watch it—I was in the middle of a game…," Yunyun objected, but I saw the edges of her mouth tug up into a hint of a smile.

And so we sat in a corner of the tavern, playing a board game.

"Hey, Megumin, have you found any party members yet?"

"No. I went on another trial quest with one adventuring group today, but they weren't able to make the most of my abilities."

"Huh. I did get one applicant, an older guy who'd already spent the whole morning drinking. He said, *'I'm just a civilian who can't even lift a sword, but if that's fine with you…'* I gave it some thought, but I decided I really need another adventurer, so I turned him down… Check."

"You should not have needed to give it *any* thought before you turned him down! What is it with you and being hit up by middle-aged men? I really worry about you sometimes… Don't go toddling after them just because they chat you up… My move, huh? I'm going to teleport my piece."

"I don't go 'toddling after' anybody—I can't be bought off with food like you, Megumin… There, it's your turn."

"I can no longer be bought off with the prospect of a mere meal. Just look—I successfully hunted a major bounty…!"

Sitting in our corner of the noisy tavern, our pieces clicked and clacked across the board as we traded barbs and complaints.

"You would think we would be mobbed by people who wanted us to join their parties just at the sight of our red eyes. Maybe all these newly minted adventurers don't understand what the Crimson Magic Clan is."

"I wonder if everyone already has a Wizard… But in school, they told us Wizards and Priests are the rarest classes, didn't they? I wonder if people are keeping their distance because of our age… Check."

"Tsk! If I pull back there, you will bring your Sword Master up, and then this square will be vulnerable to your Archer... I am going to teleport my piece here. This town doesn't appear to have many people who look like wizards of any description. I would expect greater demand."

I had noticed some people taking note of our crimson eyes, but none of them came to talk to us. Maybe Yunyun was right, and they just felt we were too young.

"That Teleport got in my way, but now it's over! You shouldn't have ignored my Adventurer just because he's the weakest piece! He's going to switch classes and become a Sword Master! Now this game is mine!"

"......*Explooosion*!"

"Ohhh!!"

I used the Arch-wizard piece's special skill—flipping the board over—and finally heaved a sigh. Maybe I would find some companions tomorrow.

"Megumin, let's play again! I want a rematch! The official rules say you can only use Explosion once per day, so next time I'm going to win! ...Hey, where are you going? You can't just run away!"

10

As I headed back to the inn, I contemplated my next move. I now had experience with two different parties. And I was starting to wonder if a wizard who could only use Explosion was not actually as useful as I'd thought.

No, no—I might not be useful to parties that aspired to hunt only weak monsters, but adventurers of a higher rank, perhaps... Yes, that was the answer: find a group that wanted to hunt large bounties, or defeat the Demon King, or fight on the front lines. They would have a place for me. There had to be someone in Axel who fit that description.

Someone seeking to defeat the Demon King.

I dragged myself along, thinking these thoughts, when I heard a pair of boisterous voices…

"Come an' get 'em! Hoppin' fresh bananas, just caught out of the river, a mere three hundred eris! Just three hundred—get 'em while they last!"

"Sweet, fresh— What? Hold on, what did you just say? Bananas, 'just caught out of the river'?"

The boy with brown hair and the girl with light-blue hair, now holding a small paper fan, were trying to move bananas in front of a produce stand.

I really seemed to run into them a lot.

"Right now, just three hundred eris! Two bunches, six hundred! …Well, that's what you would expect, but listen to this! Right this very moment, we're having a special: two bunches for just five hundred eris! Those are huge savings!"

"Y-yeah, huge! …Listen, did you really say these bananas came out of a river…?"

I guess after losing their jobs at the tavern, they'd gotten work as roadside hawkers. Apparently energized by the gathering crowd of onlookers, the girl with the blue hair raised her voice even louder and started gesturing emphatically with her fan. "Come and look, come and see, come and behold! Right now, I'm going to make these bananas *disappear*!"

"Whoa, can you do that?! Look at all these people—you're gonna look pretty dumb if you screw up, you know?!"

Intrigued, I stopped to watch.

"There are no tricks involved, nothing up my sleeve! I put this cloth over the bananas like so! Then I intone, 'Disappear! Disappear! Disappeaaaarrr'…and ta-daa!"

""""""Wowwwww!"""""""

The onlookers gasped and exclaimed; even I couldn't hold back a cry of surprise. When the girl pulled the cloth away, every single one of the bananas had vanished.

"That's *incredible*!"

"I've never seen someone pull off a trick like that!"

"Hey, I'll take one! Give me a banana!"

"Yeah, count me in!"

"Two bunches, please!"

The onlookers quickly turned into customers, practically stampeding toward the blue-haired girl.

"Thank you, thank you very much! Hoo boy, at this rate, we'll hit our quota and then some! Okay, bring back the bananas! The next time they disappear, it's gonna be because we're sold out!" The brown-haired boy was practically gleeful, but now the blue-haired girl looked at him as if confused.

"What are you talking about? I made them *disappear*. They're *gone*. Get me some more bananas so I can sell them!"

"What?! You aren't making any sense! What do you mean, 'they're gone'? Bananas don't just disappear! Where are you hiding them? Quit with the jokes and make with the bananas!"

"I'm not joking. I said there was no trick involved. Come on—hurry up and bring me some more bananas. Some to sell and some more to make disappear."

"Don't screw with me—it's past noon, so why do you sound like you're dreaming?!"

As the customers stood and watched, both of the hawkers received a solid clap on the shoulder. The owner of the produce stand was there, looking quite upset.

"You're fired."

"But whyyyyy?!"

"No, wait, let's talk it out—I didn't have anything to do with this, okay?! She's the one who made your bananas disappear!"

The girl burst into tears, and the guy tried desperately to defend himself.

The lively exchange made me realize how silly I had been to worry; I turned and headed on to the inn.

The Hunt of a Lonely Girl

I fretted away by myself in a corner of the Adventurers Guild, trying to be discreet as I kept one eye on the flyer I had made seeking party members.

Megumin, the frie—I mean, rival I had come here with, had promptly found her own companions and gone off on a quest. Our very first day as adventurers, and I could already see the huge difference between us. Megumin was an oddball, short-tempered and always spoiling for a fight, but even so, she was surprisingly social. By comparison, I had probably talked more with my pet moss ball over the course of my life than with any other human being.

For someone like me, the difficulty rating of talking to complete strangers was just too high. I had tried a few times but eventually gave up. And so I was reduced to posting a piece of paper on the board and waiting for someone to bite…

"…! I saw that! That person just now—they looked at my post!!"

When I next glanced at the bulletin board, I saw an adventuring party reading my post. Maybe, just maybe, they would let me into their group, but I needed something to say and I hadn't thought of anything to say oh stupid me, start with your name and then say your class and your special skills…!

The blood was already rushing to my head when I saw them

point to my post and nod at one another, then look around as if searching for someone—they almost looked excited about it…

When their eyes met mine, though, they shivered and looked away. The whole party seemed to shrink as they slunk out of the building. Maybe they weren't looking for party members after all…

But it was all right; I had written clearly in the post that I was an Arch-wizard. Surely, eventually, some party would come along…!

But nobody did.

Several more parties looked at my flyer after that, but for some reason, the moment they looked me in the eye, each of them quietly went away.

…After a while, a woman with glasses came over to my table.

"*A-ahem…* Pardon me, young lady, may I speak to you?"

"Y-yes, of course! How can I help you?! My name is Yunyun, and I'm an Arch-wizard but I can still only use intermediate magic so I'm very sorry about that but it's okay because I'll be able to learn advanced magic very, very soon!"

"D-don't misunderstand, please—I'm a Guild employee! I'm sorry; I'm not here because of your flyer!"

Oh. So she was someone on staff.

"U-um, is something the matter? Is there a problem with my post…?"

"N-no, although I have my questions about what you wrote there, but…we've had some complaints about a girl giving the evil eye to everyone who looks at the seeking-group board…"

It's not the evil eye; I was just curious!

"I understand there aren't that many adventurers worthy of working with someone from the Crimson Magic Clan, but, er, I must ask you to stop looking at everyone you don't like with that terrifying red gleam in your eye…"

It's not that I don't like them—that's just what happens when a Crimson Magic Clan member feels emotional!

I was so happy to think that someone might actually talk to me.

"I… I'm very sorry. I'll try to be careful…"

That made the employee look relieved. It also made her go away.

…I was a little shocked to discover people were afraid of me. I slumped face-first against the table, feeling depressed, when…

"You say you're thirteen?" I heard a voice from over my head and looked up. "'Sup? That's what the kids say, right? I should know, because I'm obviously thirteen, too! You're looking for someone to fight on the front line, right? Just leave it to me—I'm a high-level Crusader! I'll keep you *so safe*!'"

Despite the man's claims, he was clearly in his forties at least—wearing heavy full-body armor, breathing too hard and talking too fast…

………………………………………………………

"…Well, all right, maybe we could start by just having a chat…"
"Really?!"

The man seemed surprised, even though he was the one who had started the conversation.

Chapter 2

The Famous Explosion Girl and the Forest-Demon Irregular

1

A rolling plain just outside town. These lands were full of minor monsters, including the overgrown frogs known as Giant Toads. But, perhaps afraid of the stalwart guards in their striking armor, none of them dared approach the town.

Here I was, just outside Axel's front gate…

"Explooosion!"
"Hey! You there, what do you think you're doing?!"

A guard rushed up to me after I had suddenly unleashed an explosion.

"Young lady, what in the world—? Yikes! First you cast a spell at random, and then you collapse? What's going on? Stay with me!" The guard supported me as I slumped over for lack of magic.

I had just enough energy to lift my head. "P-pleased to meet you… I am Megumin of the Crimson Magic Clan, and I recently moved to this town. I believe I will be setting off many more explosions in the coming days, so we will be seeing…a good deal of…each other…"

"Oh, come on!" the guard groaned. "At least save your magic for when there are actual monsters around! Don't just set off explosions for no reason!"

I tottered back into town, carrying Chomusuke in my weak, MP-less arms. The explosion helped dispel somewhat the gloom I had been feeling recently; I walked along mumbling to myself.

"Another day with no new seeking-group flyers. What could be going on? Could it possibly be that every adventuring group in town already has all the wizards they need...?"

A week had passed since I had arrived in this town. And recently, there had been no posts at all seeking wizards. The only thing left on the board was Yunyun's flyer that she was hoping would get her either party members or friends. (I still couldn't tell which.)

Wizards were a comparatively rare class to begin with. I couldn't imagine demand had dried up so quickly...

Feeling better after I relieved some stress with my explosion, I arrived at the Adventurers Guild. It was afternoon, the time when most adventurers were out making money. And I, once again, was slumped over a table at the Guild.

"What should I do...?" I sighed. Over the course of this week, I had joined more than one party and gone on more than one quest, but...at the end of each one, the parties had acted unimpressed and refused to allow me to join them.

Nobody, it seemed, needed a wizard who could use only Explosion. Nobody needed me.

Me!

The one who had been called a genius.

"Meeeeeee!"

"Eeeek! Gosh, Megumin, don't just scream out of nowhere! I'm putting together my masterpiece here!"

Yunyun did not take kindly to my throat-scratching, hair-pulling shout, evacuating the table where she had been entertaining herself. It looked like she hadn't had any more luck finding a party than I had. She was constructing a house of cards on the table, her face scrunched seriously, taking ever so much care not to knock it down.

I had to say, Yunyun had gotten very good at entertaining herself lately. In fact, maybe people were politely steering clear of her because she looked so absorbed in what she was doing.

I picked up Chomusuke where she had curled up at my feet and set her on the table. She seemed very interested in the card Yunyun was holding in her trembling hand. She trotted over to the house of cards, and…

"Mrrrow."

"Ahhhh!"

My inky-black magical beast was evidently unable to control the waves of destruction that emanated from her, because she immediately destroyed Yunyun's masterpiece.

But who was going to blame the cat?

I gave Chomusuke a congratulatory pat on the head. She seemed quite pleased with her destruction of the little mountain of cards.

"I really don't know what I am going to do…"

"Well, you can start by apologizing to me!"

Yunyun was yammering about something, but I ignored her, lost in my own thoughts.

2

"That reminds me. Megumin, have you heard? They say they've put out a bounty on that demon who showed up in the woods." Yunyun eagerly cut the deck.

This was something that, strapped for cash as I was, I couldn't afford not to investigate.

"Oh-ho... Tell me more."

"That forest, see, it used to be full of monsters. But most of them were wiped out a long time ago. Ever since then, the only monsters left have hidden deep in the woods and don't come anywhere near town... Except, apparently, they've started showing up a lot closer to Axel just recently... That's made the woods a tempting hunting ground again. Rumor has it, though, that maybe it's that demon that's driven the other monsters so close to town."

...Monsters from the woods spilling out right up next to town? I thought I remembered a very similar phenomenon occurring near Crimson Magic Village. Could the monsters have come out because they were scared of the demon?

I remembered how a demon named Arnes had used the fear she inspired in other monsters along our travel route to drive them toward us. Was this her doing again? Perhaps not—I highly doubted she could have withstood my heartfelt explosion...

It didn't seem likely that this incident had anything to do with me specifically, but I still had a nagging feeling.

"Yunyun, about this demon. Do any of the rumors describe its appearance...?"

Just as I was asking that:

* * *

"Ooooh, look who's got himself two cute girls. Just a newb and he's already got a harem? You're makin' me jealous—toss one of those sweet things my way; you don't need 'em both!"

The Guild practically reverberated with dialogue that sounded like it belonged to some simpering plot fodder.

"Geez, what's wrong with you?!"

"Get away from us, you drunk!"

The voices must have belonged to the women in question.

When Yunyun glanced in the direction of the commotion, I said, "Don't! Yunyun, you must not meet the eyes of the likes of them, or we will get drawn into this."

"M-Megumin, how can you live with yourself?! Don't you want to try to help them?!"

She was welcome to criticize me, but this was the Adventurers Guild. This kind of scuffle was the daily bread of many of the rough-and-tumble types who came through here. It seemed a novice was involved this time; well, consider it his baptism as an adventurer.

However...

"Hmm, what do we have here...? I'm actually not a newbie. I admit I don't look like much, but I like to think I'm fairly well-known... I'm in this town hoping to find a priest who'll join my party. I don't see any around the Guild here, so I'm just heading back to my inn..." The voice sounded downright composed.

"Whazzat? 'Fairly well-known'? Then how come I don't know ya? I'm *fairly* well-known around this town myself!"

"Yeah, for all the wrong reasons. C'mon—leave him alone, man. He looks like a Sword Master or something. That's an enchanted blade he's got. I can feel crazy magic coming from it." This new voice must have belonged to one of the friends of the man who was busy getting himself in trouble. It sounded like a girl trying to stop them, but...

"Aww, shaddup, Lin! I'm not scared of any enchanted sword! Hey, you, do me a solid! You're some big-name adventurer, right? Help me out with a little training, then!"

"...Indeed, it seems I have no choice. Let's step outside, then. You two, go rest up at the inn."

"Okay. We'll meet you there once you finish off this lowlife—don't take too long."

"He looks like he'd fight dirty. Watch out, okay?"

That settled things, it seemed like. With the eyes of the entire Guild on them, the perpetrators left the building. Thinking this seemed poised to go somewhere interesting, I trotted after them for a look, but...

"Hold on, Megumin! You said it yourself—you shouldn't lock eyes with the likes of them!" Yunyun was shouting as softly as she could, being very careful not to look in the troublemakers' direction as she rained on my parade.

"But this seems set for a fascinating denouement. Don't stop me from seeing what happens."

"N-no, you can't! It's obvious who's going to win. In a few minutes, that punk is going to come back crying. And if your eyes meet his..."

"D-dammit, he must be cheating... Handsome *and* strong? Screw him. And screw all of you! What're you looking at? This ain't the zoo!"

He really did come right back. Apparently, he had barely lasted a moment after they left the Guild.

"I told you to quit while you were ahead. I know you have a dirty personality, and I can't stop you from getting into fights...but you could at least learn to pick on people your own size."

"G-geez, I get it; I'll find someone a little weaker next time... Some pigeon from the weakest class with a bunch of good-looking ladies..."

That didn't sound promising at all. I managed not to meet the punk's eyes even once. Then Yunyun and I decided to hightail it out of the Adventurers Guild before we somehow got involved.

3

The next day.

"*Explooosion*!!"

"Not you agaaaaaain!"

The guard shouted so loudly, he could practically be heard over my explosion as it echoed across the field. For the second day in a row, I had come to unleash my magic…

"Hey, you, what did I say yesterday? Don't go firing off spells for no reason! Hang on. All those craters that have been appearing near town—are you responsible for those?! Do you know how much work it'll be to fill those back in?"

"B-but I did just as you said yesterday. I have unleashed my explosion against monsters. Specifically, I eliminated a single Giant Toad! …That said, could you help me up?" At the moment, I was facedown in the dirt.

The guard sighed and picked me up. "Listen, even I can handle a frog. I'll take care of any amphibians that get too close to the gates, so maybe you could fire your magic at something farther away from town."

"I am afraid that once I cast my spell, I can no longer move. If I was paralyzed too far from town, I would be easy pickings for any monsters who happened by."

"…Seems to me like you need to find some companions, young lady."

If I could find companions, I wouldn't be in this position…

I said my farewells to the guard and once again dragged my MP-less body toward the Guild.

*   *   *

I heard a voice—one that was starting to sound awfully familiar.

"Nooooo! I caaaaaan't! Why me?! Why should I, of all people, be reduced to civil engineering?! Find a job more suited to me!"

"Gee, sorry manual labor is such a problem for you, but we need work that pays by the day and pays well—and this is the only thing left. So keep the whining to yourself!"

"Noooooo! How about another job in sales? Please let me try being a saleswoman again! This time I'm sure it'll work out!"

"And where exactly are you getting this confidence from? Come on! I don't want to do this sort of thing, either—I would love to just grab a quest and get going. But with our equipment, we'd be dead in five minutes. Okay? Beggars can't be choosers; let's at least give it a shot. It sounds like the town has been desperate for laborers out on the plain recently. Perfect time to make some cash. Don't worry—for you, it'll be easy!"

It was those two young people again, the ones I seemed to keep running into for some reason. They were outside the town's Department of Civil Engineering, arguing. It looked like they had struck out with yet another job. They must have come here when they heard about the demand for manual workers. The girl with the blue hair, however, absolutely refused to go inside.

Hmm. So it seemed I wasn't the only one lacking employment because society appeared to see no need for me.

"Don't be stupid, idiot! Just who do you think I am?! I'm not made for dusty, dirty physical work! And it's about time I had some real gourmet food! It's been bread crusts every day! Why should I have to eat like that?! A being as exalted as I am needs to take care what she eats!"

"You were eating potato chips when I met you! Now stop whining, and let's get going! I want to earn some equipment and get adventuring!"

"Noooooo! I hate civil engineering! How can a socially withdrawn loser like you be so proactive?!"

They were like me—just doing everything they could to scrape by. I watched the young man drag the girl away before I headed to the Adventurers Guild to find some work of my own.

4

Several adventurers got to their feet when they saw me enter the Guild. Almost like they were afraid of me. Could it be because I was Crimson Magic Clan? Or was it because I had acquired the gravitas of a true adventurer?

The thought made me smirk, but then I saw the adventurers who had stood up go over to the bulletin board and tear down several flyers.

....

"Excuse me."

"Y-yes?! Can I help you?!"

I was speaking to one of the adventurers who had torn something off the board; she seemed unduly worried.

"…Ma'am, could I perhaps have a look at that flyer you just tore down?"

"Uh… No."

"Gimme!" I grabbed the piece of paper from where she had tried to hide it behind her back. Whereupon…

Wizard wanted. Four-person party. Any spells okay.

"Oh-ho! *Any* spells, I see! How convenient! I just so happen to be a wizard in between parties myself!"

"S-s-sorry, spot's filled; we found our newest member just a moment ago, and that's why I was removing our post…!"

The woman tried to get away, but I grabbed her. "I have had quite enough of these excuses! What is this, anti-Explosion discrimination? Is this entire Guild conspiring to shun me?!"

"D-don't get the wrong idea! No one is discriminating against Explosion; it's just recently… There's been this girl who knows Explosion, and she's really… Like, the moment she sees a monster, it's *bam!* Explosion! According to the rumors, she's a real nutjob…"

"I believe those are fighting words! Let us see how much you can bad-mouth me *after* you witness my explosion! …Hey, what are you—? Stop that!"

"No magic inside the building!"

I had begun to intone my spell despite the fact that I was out of MP, and I soon found myself overpowered by an assortment of staff and adventurers and dragged into another room.

"Miss Megumin, this just won't do. Anything more powerful than advanced magic is forbidden in town. The next time we catch you trying to use magic around here, you'll be locked up for a whole night."

Maybe it was a sign of how far I had sunk that my first thought was to file that threat away for when I was out of money and really needed a place to stay.

Having suffered my scolding by the Guild staff, I went over to where Yunyun was entertaining herself…

"N-no way! Do you think I'm so easy, I would just go toddling after anyone at all?!"

"No, I don't! I'm just asking you! I swear I don't have any ulterior motives! All I want is to get my mom off my back, so I need you to pretend to be my girlfriend for a while! My poor, sick mother says she wants to see her grandchild's face before she dies…! Or if that's not possible, at least see her son's wife…! I'm turning to the only person I could lean on at a time like this, my one and only friend, you, Yunyun…!"

A man I didn't recognize in the least bowed repeatedly, begging Yunyun to do…something or other for him.

"O-only friend... Ugh, but—pretending to be your girlfriend...?! I'm only thirteen! I'm still a minor!" she rejected.

"That doesn't matter—I just need you to poke your head in and say hello to her!" the man said. "Don't worry—you don't have to do anything! It'll be fine!"

"Really?! H-hold on. Why do you sound so desperate?! I really don't think I can—"

"*Pleeeease!* I'm begging you, just a date, just an hour—just thirty minutes!" The man sounded downright tragic, practically worshipping Yunyun now.

"But wait, that's not what you said before...! I thought I was only supposed to pretend for your sick mother?! How did that turn into a date...?"

"Pleeeaaassse, please, please, please!" The man was begging on his hands and knees.

"Wait, hold on, just wait a moment..."

"Please, please, please, please! You see how it is, and I'm begging you, just a little, I'm begging you!!"

Finally worn down, Yunyun, looking more than a little apprehensive, said to the kneeling man, "Urrrgh... W-well, maybe if it's only...j-just for a little while!"

"You'll do it?!"

"Of course she won't do it. Who do you think you are, taking advantage of people's kindness! I'm going to call the police on you!"

"Wh-who the heck are you?! Wait— Oh! You've got to be that crazy—! No, stop, don't call the cops! Anything but that! I get it! I'll go away—I promise!"

And true to his word, he went dashing off.

I made a shooing motion in his direction as I went over to Yunyun. "*What* do you think you are doing?! I cannot believe you, getting swept along so easily! No good can come of letting him pull you into his little games!"

"A-awww, but, but! His sick mother, she just wanted to see—"

"That's a low-down lie! What else?! Did anyone ask you to do anything else shady while I was away?!"

"N-nobody asked me to do anything shady! The only person who asked me to do anything was that old man who drinks here every day. He said, *'Start calling me Daddy, sweetheart.'* But that was it…"

"That sounds like the very definition of shady! You turned him down, right?! Listen to me: If that old fart talks to you again, don't give him the time of day! If your real father, the chief of our clan, found out that his daughter was in a far-off city calling strange men Daddy, he would burst into tears!"

Yunyun was so immensely, desperately vulnerable. Look at all the trouble she had managed to get herself caught up in just a week after we had arrived.

Yunyun only pulled out a piece of paper and studied it. "What else am I supposed to do? I spend all day, every day by myself in this tavern—if someone wants to talk to me, why, I would hardly even care if they were a recruiter for the Axis Church…"

"What do you have there? Throw that away—you don't need that!" I grabbed the Axis profession of faith from Yunyun, wadded it up, and tossed it aside.

This would never do. I had been leaving Yunyun to fend for herself in the hopes that it would cure her of her shyness, but she was too far gone in her loneliness, and it was taking her to some dangerous places.

But I had my hands full looking for an adventuring party…

It hit me in a flash.

"Yunyun. How about this: You and I can form a party temporarily—until we both find parties of our own."

"Whaaaaaaaaat?!"

Yunyun really seemed more surprised than necessary by my invitation. Was it that strange?

"But! B-b-but…! I made a resolution…! I made a declaration, and it's hardly been a week since then…"

Hmm? I had no idea what Yunyun was talking about.

"What is the matter? I am only suggesting we form a party together—why should it cause you such consternation?"

Yunyun scrunched up her face. "…H-hey, Megumin. You remember what I said, don't you? You know, about…about how we were going to settle things once I learned advanced magic?"

"Oh, you mean your mutterings in the carriage after we finished off Arnes. What about them?"

I thought I was encouraging her to go on, but Yunyun looked like she might burst into tears. "What do you mean, 'what about them'…? I can't *believe* this! We make an important promise, and it just pops right out of your head! This is how it always is with you, Megumin! How can you claim to be the greatest genius of the Crimson Magic Clan when you're just a dummy who can't remember one single important thing?!"

"Say *what*?!"

"Yikes, no fighting in the building!"

For the second time that day, I, along with Yunyun, found myself being lectured by a Guild employee, after which we were summarily ejected from the building.

5

"Ugh! Megumin, why are you always like this?! Do you never learn? Has the shock wave from those explosions scrambled your brain so badly that you have permanent amnesia?"

"You *still* have a bone to pick with me? And now that we are outside, there is no one to stop me from going berserk!"

"Wh-what, you want to fight?! You're so low on MP, you can hardly stand up, and you still think you can beat me?!"

We were on our way back to the inn. And we were still at each other's throats.

"Argh…! That was the declaration of a lifetime, and you don't even remember…! I can't believe you; I just can't!" Yunyun buried her face in her hands and shook her head vigorously.

"Fine, I understand. It was wrong of me to forget. So what? What was this all-important vow that you made? Repeat it for me."

"What?!" Yunyun went bright red.

"I do not think what I said was that difficult. But to reiterate, what was this vow that was so important to you? I promise I'm listening now. Go ahead." I walked slightly off the road, just into the underbrush, and assumed a formal sitting position to show how seriously I was attending to her.

That only seemed to throw Yunyun off even more. "L-look, it's nothing, okay? It doesn't matter anymore—just forget about it, for real this time! We'll talk about it some other time."

"Excuse me. What do you mean, then, by going around calling people dummies? I do not know what has you so embarrassed, but hurry up and come out with it. I will certainly listen now."

Yunyun, confronted with my serious listening pose, looked almost tearful. But then she scrunched up her face with resolve…!

"It was, well… O-once I learn advanced magic, once I'm not going to slow you down anymore—! Then you and I—"

"Excuse me, you there!! May I trouble you for a moment?"

A middle-aged butler in a coat with tails interrupted Yunyun.

"You certainly may not. We were just getting to the good part; go away!"

"P-please hear me out! I am looking for someone!" he said. Yunyun and I glanced at each other. "It so happens that a young lady of our household has run away to escape an arranged marriage… I'm very sorry to trouble two strangers with this business, but please help me search for her…! In this land, beautiful golden hair and blue eyes are the sign of a pure-blooded noble. Our young lady has golden hair that stretches all the way down her back. If you see anyone fitting her description, please be so kind as to inform the Dustiness household. I assure you, we will be certain to show our gratitude…!" Then the middle-aged man bowed politely.

The Dustiness household—they were a noble family so prominent that even I, with my minimum of experience of the world, knew who they were. A young woman who had run away from her family was a serious thing indeed. The man's description of her conjured up a gorgeous, refined person. No doubt she was elegant, with a delicate figure. A sweet young girl at heart—I was interested in seeing such a proper young lady for myself and even more interested in the proffered reward.

"Please leave it to us," I said. "If we see any such person, we will certainly bring her to you."

"Thank you so much! It would mean the world to us!" Then the butler went running after another passerby.

"Yunyun, let us go! Seeing how our wallets are empty, finding that poor, lost lamb of a noble girl should be our first priority!"

"U-uh…! I'm not especially lacking in money…!"

I dragged Yunyun along as I went running off!

"So tired… And we never found the noble girl…"

"Tsk…! And here I ran all over town in hopes of a nice, fat reward from House Dustiness! Where *could* that girl be hiding…?"

We had turned the town inside out but had come back to our inn without having found so much as a clue to the whereabouts of the missing girl.

We were dealing with a child of nobility. Getting out of the house would be easy enough, but once in the outside world, she would have no idea what to do. She was probably hiding somewhere, paralyzed with fright. Or worse, maybe an awful man had dragged her off someplace.

Gold hair and blue eyes was such an unusual combination that I had thought for sure we would find her right away, but the only person we saw with gold hair around Axel was some lady in filthy armor, traveling with a silver-haired Thief and yammering something about how a demon had appeared in the forest and she was going to "beat the living crap out of it" in the name of the goddess Eris.

No matter how hard we searched, there was no sign of a refined young noblewoman anywhere.

"…It seems we must admit defeat. I should not have relied on the vagaries of fortune! Starting tomorrow, we will take up a proper quest!"

"So are we really starting a party?! Come on—after I was so serious about the whole learning-advanced-magic thing! You know, it took me a lot of courage to say all that! Do you really not remember?!"

6

The next morning. We were happy that there weren't too many adventurers at the Guild when we arrived early that day—it gave us a chance to have a close look at all the quests on the bulletin board.

Chomusuke was back in my room, Yunyun and I having decided that we wouldn't be able to protect her in case of a monster attack.

"Megumin, how about we start with something simple?" Yunyun said, holding up a post representing the bread and butter of adventuring in this town, a Giant Toad hunt. These extremely fecund frogs were also an essential part of the food chain in Axel.

I mentally put it in the "maybe" pile as I scanned the other posts…

Clean Gravestones by the Mansion on the Outskirts of Town

Laborers Wanted to Fill in Craters on Plain

Common Graveyard: Zombie Maker Hunt

Seeking Runaway Young Noblewoman

Lake Water Quality Inspection: The recent uptick in civil engineering projects has resulted in leftover silt and dirt washing into the lake.

And so on and so forth…

Hmm, this posed a riddle. We were a party of two wizards. The ideal quest for us would be a hunt mission demanding considerable firepower.

"Then perhaps we should go where rumor says all the tastiest stuff is—into the forest."

"What?! You mean the forest, where there's supposed to be a demon so big and so bad that they put a bounty on its head?! There's only two of us! Let's start with some nice, easy monsters on the plain!"

That demon with the huge bounty was exactly what I was after. But I knew better than to tell Yunyun that, lest she decide to spend another day sitting by herself in the Guild. Fine, we could go to the stupid plain first, if that was what she needed to build up some confidence…!

"Ah, brought a friend today, Miss? That's good, that's great, now you'll be just fine. Get *plenty* of distance from town, and then you can fire off magic to your heart's content." As we exited the town gate, I had to suffer the condescension of the guardsman. It seemed he already remembered who I was.

Not far outside of town, Yunyun's eyes began to sparkle. "G-gosh, Megumin, you've been so busy that the guard already knows who you are? And here I thought you had just been killing time."

"Th-that is quite enough! Don't pretend I am like you, with your communication impediment. While you have been playing in a corner by yourself, I have already succeeded in establishing something of a reputation for myself in this town. Why, even at the Adventurers Guild, there are more than a few who know me by sight."

"What?! Since when?!"

I ignored Yunyun's shock and went in search of my prey.

...Nothing I'd said was untrue.

"*Fireball*!" Yunyun's magic exploded against the frog, which had been sitting lazily on the plain. It was nothing next to Explosion, but it made a fairly decent boom, and it successfully fried the frog. My stomach rumbled a little at the appetizing aroma of cooking frog flesh.

"Yunyun... You don't happen to have any salt with you, do you?"

"What, you want to sit down and eat right here?! No, we need to take this frog back to the Guild and sell it to them. Subtract transport fees, and the frogs get us five thousand eris each. And if we take out five of them, there's a quest completion bonus, too—I'd say that's pretty good."

I looked longingly at the blackened frog. Three of them, in total, lay collapsed on the ground. That represented a total of fifteen thousand eris. Two more, and we would allegedly get a hundred-thousand-eris completion bonus as well. I had heard frog hunts were pretty standard work, and I had to admit, I was impressed by the rate of return.

It wasn't bad, and yet...

"Very well. I think you should be feeling reasonably confident by now. Let us alert the Guild to pick up these frogs, and then we shall proceed to the forest."

"What, so soon?! We only just finished our first battle!" Yunyun objected.

"Yes, and what has it proven to us? It shows precisely how strong the magic of the Crimson Magic Clan is. These minor pests are beneath us; we should seek out a stronger foe. Your level will never increase if you spend all your time picking off small fries."

"Okay, that's a fair point, but, Megumin, you didn't do anything! Be honest: Am I the only one of us who can actually fight? I can't help feeling like if we go into the woods, we're bound to run into that demon everyone's talking about…"

"And that would be ideal. Just think about it for two seconds. I defeated Arnes, did I not? She may have had a few screws loose, but she was still a high-level demon. Compared with her, some random fiend haunting the woods is nothing. You just handle the minor enemies, Yunyun, and if the big bad shows up, leave it to me. How does that sound?"

Despite my confidence, Yunyun scrunched her nose, sensing something fishy. "Well…maybe it would be all right. Even though I know that the more confident you are, Megumin, the worse things seem to go…"

"Y-you are very sassy today! Look, consider that if we exterminate this notorious demon, the other adventurers will certainly be grateful to us. Imagine that day, all the parties that will invite you to join them…"

"……I'll go."

And so we went.

7

We proceeded assiduously into the dim, overgrown forest, Yunyun ahead and me behind. So far, everything was going well; we hadn't encountered any monsters to speak of.

"The last time I was in these woods, we were beset by slimes and assailed by flying squirrels, yet today there is no sign of any of them."

"Flying squirrels? There are flying squirrels in this forest? Ooh, flying squirrels are kinda cute, aren't they?"

Yunyun, blissfully unaware of the true terror of those monsters, was enjoying the thought. Meanwhile, I was thinking she could do with getting some squirrel pee on *her* head.

The bushes just in front of us rustled, and I cried out. "L-look! You've called them forth by talking about them!"

Yunyun was immediately on the alert, drawing both her wand and her dagger from her belt. In front of us appeared—!

"I-it's so cute…!!" Yunyun breathed, her eyes sparkling.

In front of us appeared a fluffy, moist-eyed bunny about the size of a puppy. The only unusual thing about it was the horn sprouting from its head. It might be cute, but I suspected it was still plenty monstrous.

"Yunyun, the Guild employee warned us specifically about this monster—the Lovely Rabbit. Don't let its cuteness fool you—keep up your guard and finish it off."

"What?! Y-you want me to kill it?! This sweet little thing?!" Yunyun was practically weeping. Despite her tearful appeal, though, this was a monster we were facing. And we were adventurers…!

"Coo…," the rabbit said. Then it cocked its fluffy head.

A—a c-cute monster was still a monster.

I must not let down my guard…!

The Lovely Rabbit came toward us at what could best be described as a toddle, approaching Yunyun at an unsteady gait.

"It's *so cute*…! Megumin, it's so cute, I can hardly stand it! It's unbelievably adorable! Megumin, there has to be some kind of mistake—this thing can't be a monster! Just look how sweet it is!"

"Keep it together, Yunyun; we were specifically warned about this creature. 'Lovely Rabbit' is just a name; I'm sure we can't be too caref—"

Before I could finish, the rabbit fixed me with its wet, red eyes.

"Coo?"

You don't like me? it seemed to be asking.

…I wanted to pet it. I wanted to give it a hug and pet all its troubles away!

"Here, sweetheart, I have a veggie stick! C'mere, sweetie!" Yunyun, already completely taken in, took out a vegetable stick that perhaps she had been planning to have for lunch and set it on the ground.

"That's no fair! I want to—"

—*feed it, too*, I was about to say, but the rabbit crept closer to Yunyun, completely ignoring the vegetable stick.

There was considerably more rustling from the bushes the bunny had come from.

""".........?""""

Yunyun and I looked at each other; then slowly we turned toward the underbrush…

Waiting there was an entire horde of white bunnies, all crouched around something. What were they doing there?

…I squinted, and then I realized what the something was.

They must have stabbed it with their sharp horns. For lying on the ground, dead from the assortment of stab wounds on its body, was a huge gray wolf. That was what the rabbits had flocked to. Meaning…

""They're carnivores?!"" we exclaimed, causing the rabbits to collectively look in our direction.

The bunny that had been waddling along a moment before got a glint in its eye, and I threw myself to the ground. A beat later, something white flew over my head. I heard a *thump* of something impacting the trunk of a tree. Slowly, fearfully, I looked back, where I saw my hat pinned to a tree trunk by a rabbit horn, with the rabbit still attached.

As the creature struggled to free itself, I ran over and wrung its neck. Then I pulled the limp rabbit out of the tree and retrieved my hat. "Yunyun, these creatures are just despicable! They pretended to be cute and then attacked us when our guards were down!!"

"All that cuteness and cooing—these monsters are nasty, nasty, nasty!"

But our complaining didn't stop the horde of rabbits from bearing down on us!

8

We managed to outrun the stampeding bunnies by the skin of our teeth, after which we found a tree stump to rest upon.

"Arrrgh, now I have a hole in my hat... I'll have to borrow a needle and thread when we get back to the inn," I moaned, clutching my hat.

"*Hff... Hff...* Th-that scared the life out of me... A species of adorable monster that forms packs to hunt and kill? Imagine the trauma a psychologically unprepared person might face..." Yunyun was breathing hard, her face pale, having used up a lot of her magic on a spell.

True, they had been fearsome foes. The way the thing had waddled toward us at first turned out to be just an act. The sheer speed of them as they chased us down...!

"We had to run away; there were too many of them. I didn't even get to bring back the rabbit I managed to defeat. We won't get any reward for rabbit meat that way."

"Are you suggesting you want to go back to those killer rabbits, Megumin? I sure don't. They might be cute, but you saw them—they were eating a *wolf.* When I saw that, I thought I was going to cry."

I sympathized. I wasn't eager to get anywhere near them again, myself.

"Megumin, how about we call it quits for today? I used up a lot of my MP in that battle. Let's at least go back and do our hunting on the plains."

I nodded slowly at Yunyun's suggestion. After a few minutes' rest, we could circle around back to town, avoiding the place where we had run into the bunnies.

"Oh, by the way, I exterminated enough of those rabbits that my level increased. At this rate, it won't be long before the day when I finally learn advanced magic." Yunyun was downright gleeful.

"…We should definitely limit our hunting to the weak enemies on the plain, starting tomorrow."

"B-but why? What, are you afraid that I'll get ahead of you? You are, aren't you? I knew it!" Yunyun was busy shaking me by the shoulders, but that was when I noticed something.

"…? Is it just me, or is something coming this way? I hear a sound."

It was a faint rumbling.

Then Yunyun heard it, too. "…? You know, I think you're right. I wonder what that is. A monster? Perfect, I'll take it out and get another level…"

"That is no fair; I get the next one. You watch and learn."

"What's this about, Megumin? I thought you were going to be our ace in the hole in case we ran into that demon. Just because you don't want me to catch up to you… Hey, does something seem weird to you?" Yunyun looked distinctly uneasy.

Yes, there was something strange, all right. The *number* of rumbles…

"I have a bad feeling about this. I think we ought to withdraw for now. The greatest warrior is she who wins without fighting and all."

"Y-yeah, I agree. I think I've had enough battles for today. Let's go home, cash in our frogs, and use the money to get some dinner."

Even as Yunyun spoke, the noise got louder. It sounded a lot like a group of monsters coming our way…!

"R-run, Yunyun! We can't win this one; we don't want to be here when they arrive!"

"Oh, wait for me, Megumin! Don't leave me here… Oh!"

The sound suddenly stopped. All that we heard in the ensuing silence was something rustling in the bushes behind us.

And then it came flying out…

A Lovely Rabbit, just like we had fought earlier.

*   *   *

Had it been chasing us, or was something chasing it? There was no hint of cuteness left in its eyes.

"""""*Coo!*"""""

The rabbits came pouring out of the underbrush, howling, red eyes gleaming.

"Megumin— Megumin, there are so many of them— *Lightning*! Wh-what do we do?!"

"T-try to buy us some time, and then I'll take them all out in one shot!" I called as Yunyun unleashed a spell on the rabbit in the vanguard. I raised my staff and began to chant.

"Won't everyone be angry if you use Explosion in the woods?! I've been purposely avoiding my Fireball spell so I don't start a forest fire! *Blade of Wind*!" Yunyun backed up, casting another spell in the meantime that swept one of the rabbits away.

Yunyun had whipped out her short sword, which crashed into the horn on a rabbit, sending sparks flying into the air.

"If I don't do this, we're going to be bunny food! Natural destruction is nothing to be afraid of, not if you want to be a master of Explosion! Yunyun, get down!"

"What?! No—! Wait…!!"

"*Explooosion*!!"

The rabbits were really too close for comfort, which meant, I knew, that they were close enough that we would feel some of the effects of the blast.

A beam of light flew from the end of my staff, landing squarely in the middle of the furry horde. There was a pause, and then a vicious blast tore up the area, trees and all.

Yunyun and I were at the mercy of the brutal blast wind…

9

"—O…o, humans… Yo, humans. You alive?"

The voice seemed so far away.

It appeared I had lost consciousness for a moment. From what I could tell, I was lying on my side on the ground. A tree branch or something was digging into my cheek, so I assumed I was still in the woods.

My eyes fluttered open, and I was confronted with Yunyun, blissfully asleep.

I gave her a good smack on the cheek. She frowned in discomfort, but I was relieved to know she was still breathing.

I wondered how long I had been out. Despite draining my MP on Explosion, I felt like I could sit up if I really wanted to, so it must have been long enough for some of my MP to regenerate.

"You awake? Those eyes—are y'all Crimson Magic Clan?"

There was that voice again, above me. Perhaps whoever was speaking had been keeping us safe while we were unconscious.

"…Oof, ow-ow-ow-ow…? Where are we? I hurt all over…" Frowning, Yunyun opened her eyes and tried to sit up.

As I made to do the same…

…I turned to our interlocutor and said, "Yes, we are from the Crimson Magic Clan. My name is Megumin, and—"

Then I saw who I was talking to and froze.

Yunyun managed to sit up, looking a bit out of it. "…? What's wrong, Megumin? You look like you've seen a ghost… Hey, wait! I remember! What's wrong with you, setting off an explosion right in front of us? Hey, are you listening…to…me…?"

Her stern rebuke trailed off as she followed my fixated gaze…

*   *   *

"Hey, 'sup? Got a minute? The name's Host, and, uh, I'm lookin' for a big, black magical beast right around here… Whoa, hey, hang on. You…you look familiar. Have we met? Nah, wait—you look like someone I know…"

A demon stood before us.

His inky-black skin reflected the light as if it were metal. His massive wings looked like they belonged to a wildly overgrown bat. He was big enough that he could have intimidated an ogre, and it was impossible to miss the twisting horns and fangs.

A high-level demon. We were locking eyes with the sort of creature you would normally see only in the very deepest depths of some final dungeon somewhere.

"…My name is Host! High-level demon—not just some overgrown goblin! He who will one day be commanded by this one kid I know! …How's about that? Little self-intro for ya. I know you're Crimson Magic folks, right? I know this is how you roll."

""Aaaahhhhhhhhhhhhhhhhhhhhhhhh!!""

One look at the demon's toothy grin sent Yunyun and me screaming in the other direction.

10

I had no idea how far we had run. We had made it out of the forest at some point, whereupon we looked back to make sure the demon wasn't following us and then collapsed into a heap. Yunyun's eyes were puffy with tears; she must have been genuinely terrified.

"*Hff… Hff…!* Wh-wha…? Wh-what the heck?! That was a demon!

A big, mean, high-level demon! I've never been so scared in my whole life…"

"*Hff… Hff…* I must admit, I underestimated the sort of demon that would be living around here. I never expected him to be quite so big…" To be frank, if I had run into that creature when I was all alone, I do believe I would have wet myself.

Arnes, my most recent demon acquaintance, had also been of a high level. But I guess the bigger they are, the more impact they have, because the demon in those woods was far scarier. Now that I had a chance to think about it, I was amazed we had escaped.

Yunyun, gradually collecting herself, said, "Megumin. Did you think it was weird, what that demon said? He was talking about the Crimson Magic Clan and a huge magical beast…"

"I don't really recall, for I had better things to do than memorizing his every word. I think he said I looked familiar… Well, in any event. We can be grateful simply to still have our lives after encountering the likes of him. I think I would prefer to stay out of the woods for a while." I let out a long breath.

Yunyun nodded, pale-faced. "I'm so tired… Come on. Let's go home and get some rest, okay?"

"Yes, perhaps we should… Oh, but before that. We need to stop by the Guild and get paid for our frogs. We can report about that demon, too."

After a few minutes' rest there on the border between the forest and the field, we headed back to town.

We had gone out early that day, but between hunting on the plains and hunting in the woods, quite a bit of time had passed.

Sunset had begun to color the scenery when we pushed open the door of the Adventurers Guild.

* * *

"It's true, I tell you! He was just staring at the abandoned castle on the hill near town! He was on this war cart pulled by a headless horse, going who knows where...!"

It must have been the hour: The Guild was abuzz with adventurers drinking and chatting. Ignoring all the shouting, we worked our way over to the reception desk.

"Excuse me. We've come to collect our reward..."

"Oh, Miss Megumin and Miss Yunyun. We've already brought in the frogs. Three frogs, fifteen thousand eris. Hold on, please." A receptionist lady prepared our payment.

"Ummm... Would there happen to be any hunt quests for Lovely Rabbits? We took out quite a few of them in the woods." I held up my Adventurer's Card, which showed the number and type of monsters I had defeated.

"Hmm, Lovely Rabbits normally don't come out of the deep woods. That means they don't usually do anyone any harm, and there aren't normally any quests for them... But they've been spotted near town often enough recently that there might be a hunt for them soon."

Hmph, too bad.

...There was one other thing, though.

"Actually, we also ran into that demon in the woods everyone's been talking about. He's very high-level. He was intelligent enough to identify himself, and he was a giant—truly intimidating. He's one serious enemy, no doubt about it."

The receptionist's face tightened at that.

"He also said something about searching for a huge, black magical beast. We were able to talk to him, and he didn't attack us, so I was thinking maybe he's a friendly demon...," Yunyun continued, but the woman shook her head.

"A pitch-black magical beast, you say? ...I can think of one such creature. It's a very dangerous monster called the Beginner's Bane—it has a large build and black fur. But I wonder why he would be looking for one of those. Maybe he wants to keep it as a pet...?" The woman thought about it for a moment.

"Oh," she added, "thank you both for the information. I just can't imagine what a high-level demon would want with a Beginner's Bane. This is beyond dangerous. Until we figure out what's going on, we may need to restrict access to the forest entirely. Don't go back in there if you don't have to," she said, and then she gave us our reward for the frogs.

11

"Gosh, it seems like this really blew up."

We were on our way back to our inn when the words came suddenly out of Yunyun's mouth.

"It was bad timing. I had just used up my magic. If I'd still had my spell, I would have iced him in one shot..."

"Stop! You can't beat an enemy like that! I think that demon could have withstood even your Explosion!"

"...Oh-ho, is that a challenge I hear? Very well, let us forget what we were planning to do tomorrow and go back to the woods..."

"No way! I am *not* going in there! If you want to go to the woods, you're going by yourself—do you hear me?!"

As we walked along, quarreling, we passed by the Department of Civil Engineering.

"Th-thanks, boss... All in a day's work..."

"Yeah, nice hustle!"

                              *   *   *

I spotted that increasingly familiar pair emerging. I guess they had just gotten off work themselves.

The man looked absolutely beat, but the girl, who had been so dead set against manual labor this morning, had a huge grin on her face and looked downright fulfilled.

Hardly able to stay on his feet, the young man said, "Hey, let's find something else to do tomorrow... You were right after all. We aren't made for civil engineering..."

"Speak for yourself," the young woman shot back. "This is the problem with a socially withdrawn NEET like you. How do you expect to get by in the world if you throw in the towel on every job after your first day? C'mon—let's take our pay and catch a nice, refreshing bath and then have something good to eat! Then we can throw ourselves into tomorrow!" She clenched her fist, her eyes practically sparkling. She seemed to have discovered the joy of hard work.

"Why did you stop? Do you know those people?"

"...No, they're complete strangers. It's nothing; let's go." I resumed following Yunyun back to our lodging. It was true: For as often as I saw them, I still didn't know those people. They always seemed to be having a good time, though. It sort of nagged at me.

"I could go for a nice, cold Crimson Beer," the blue-haired girl said.

"H-hold on, is that some kind of alcohol? Are we allowed to drink around here? What does the law say in this country?"

"Pfft, scaredy-cat. Fine, I'll get by with an ice-cold Neroid for today."

"Neroid? The heck is that?"

The woman didn't bother to answer. "I'm so hungry—let's get a move on! The public baths start opening about this time; did you know that? We might be the first ones in the tub at this hour! I'm gonna get going!" No sooner had she finished speaking than she rushed off.

"Whoa! Hey, wait up! What the heck is a Neroid?! If you keep running, you're gonna fall down ag—"

Before the young man even finished speaking, the girl went tumbling.

"…Megumin, I think you'd better not watch them too closely…"

"Y-yes, I think you are right. Let us be going."

I could hear the young woman behind me, crying about where her purse with her day's pay had gone when she fell.

As for Yunyun and me, we went back to our inn.

I couldn't believe how much had happened today. Finding a quest with Yunyun, hunting frogs and then finally bunnies.

And then meeting a very powerful demon.

…Who *was* that creature anyway? The moment he saw me, he said I looked like someone he knew… If I recalled correctly, he was looking for a massive, pitch-black magical beast. Honestly, I was starting to wish we had taken a few more minutes to talk to him.

These thoughts ran through my head as I opened my door and walked into my room…

…and immediately ran out again, rushing over to knock on Yunyun's door.

"Yunyun! I'm sorry, but you must come here immediately! It's Chomusuke! My tiny, pitch-black magical beast is practically dead!"

"Did you feed her?! We've been out all day, and she's just been shut up in here! You left food and water out for her, right?!"

The Worries of a Lonely Girl

"Listen up, you two! You want an adventuring companion? I've got just the guy! Lain Sheyka! He's an unbelievably talented spearman, and he's right here in town! He was the youngest person ever to attain the rank of Dragon Knight the next country over, and he's supposed to be *so* famous…!"

"I dunno, y'know? Smells fishy to me—what's a living legend doing in a town full of newbies? Heck, do you even know what he looks like?"

"Er… W-well… No, not exactly, but I've heard he's a noble by birth! And all nobles, other than the ones who have bought their position with money, have golden hair and blue eyes! We just have to look around until we find the blond, blue-eyed, and totally dignified hottie, and we'll have him!"

I could hear the girls jabbering from across the Adventurers Guild. When I looked over, I saw a young woman carrying a spear and another who looked like a Thief. They both looked about my age.

"A great spearman, huh? You're right—gold hair would definitely stand out. Honestly, though, I think I'd rather have a wizard or a priest—if we see anyone like that, let's talk to them." The speaker smiled at the two women: He was a young guy carrying what looked like an enchanted sword. I guess the three of them were in a party together.

What really interested me, though, was what the young man had just said about wanting a wizard…

This could be my chance. If I just sat here waiting for something to happen to me, the gulf between Megumin and me would only grow. I had already given up once on trying to initiate conversations with adventurers, but if I didn't do something now, I was sure I would regret it. I wasn't going to play second fiddle to Megumin forever!

I got up my nerve and then stood, starting over toward the young man…

"Grr!"

"Hiss!"

…until I was cut off by the two women, who gave me unmistakably threatening looks. I turned around and went right back to my seat.

I had failed. A forlorn coward like me was doomed to be second fiddle my entire life.

But that was when it happened.

"You there. You're worried about something, yes? I may not look it, but I am a priest. If you wish, I would be happy to listen to your concerns."

As I sat there, slumped on the table, having failed yet again at getting companions and wishing I could just die, a lovely woman, a little older than me, came and talked to me. She wore a robe mostly of blue—probably an Axis follower, I figured. I had run into a lot of trouble with them in the last city we'd been in, and I wasn't really eager to have anything more to do with them, but…

"…You know, I thought I could manage *something* if I came to this town, but not a single thing has gone right, and it's just killing me…"

Before I knew what I was doing, I was baring my soul to the older woman. Even though she was one of those terrifying Axis followers who hounded people with their so-called freedom.

She listened silently and then said, "It's all right. For verily, even unto you, Lady Aqua reaches out her hand of salvation."

I found myself looking up hopefully at the young woman's kind words. I gazed at her beseechingly, and she produced a single sheet of paper. It looked familiar.

Axis Church Profession of Faith.

"Now, if you will only join the Axis Church, you will surely make a friend…!" Suddenly, she was on the attack, trying to shove the paper into my hands…!

"G-geez, how low can you go? I didn't think even the Axis Church would try to take advantage of a girl so down in the dumps. Set 'em up and knock 'em down! Look at her smile!"

"I know their religion is, like, to do the worst things they can to people, but I can't believe this… And that girl is buying it…"

I could hear people whispering about us from a distance.

I grabbed the profession of faith.

"I *will* join the Axis Church! And then… Then I'll have friends and companions and everything, right?!"

""""Buh?""""

Everyone sounded completely flabbergasted—including, for some reason, the young woman from the Axis Church.

The God-Awful Priest and the Goddess of Water

1

The Guild was in an uproar this morning.

"Three different parties need Priests! Would any parties with two or more Priests please send one over here?"

"Any Wizards around?! We don't have enough potions, and we need someone who can make some!"

It had been a week since I had reported to the Guild about that demon. The forest had been declared off-limits while an investigation was conducted, and as adventurers, we lost one of our cushiest hunting grounds. At first, everyone had obediently gone hunting in the plains instead. But hot-blooded adventurers could never follow instructions for too long.

The Guild, plagued by questions of when people would be allowed in the woods again, decided to hunt down the demon and began assembling a task force for that purpose. Anyone who was confident enough had been preparing all morning, many of them looking to work off some frustration over the loss of their hunting ground.

I observed the busy scene in the Guild.

"Seems we have quite a commotion on our hands again," I remarked to Yunyun, who was clutching her wand and looking very nervous.

"H-how can you be so calm?! You saw that thing, Megumin—that demon! Crimson Magic Village is full of powerful monsters, and even it doesn't have anything that nasty!" She seemed caught between criticizing me and bursting into tears.

"If you are so against the idea, you can certainly just stay here, yes? With this many adventurers, though, I don't believe we will ever be caught out. We're nowhere near a hundred people, but we will have well more than twenty or thirty. We will get a reward simply for being part of this hunting group. Even someone toddling along at the back would get at least a little pocket change, so this is not an opportunity to miss."

"G-gosh, really…! W-well, if you're going to be a part of it, Megumin, I certainly can't let you go alone…"

"I'm sorry—did you say something? You did, didn't you? Come on! Say it so I can hear."

"You heard me perfectly well, didn't you?! What's the big idea, trying to get me to repeat what you already heard?!" Yunyun pressed herself against the table, hands to her face, red up to her ears. I smirked and gave her a good shake before looking around the Guild again.

According to Yunyun, who had apparently been here all morning, an attractive woman slightly older than us (but of poor pallor) had come by with an armload of potions. She had, I was told, mournfully mumbled, *"I guess this means bread crusts and sugar water for me for a while…"* as she handed them over.

With this many people and this much support, I figured we would be safe even against that demon.

"Truthfully, though, the reward money isn't the only reason we should want to participate in this hunt. Think about it. If we show what we can do on this job, we won't have to go around asking people if we can join their parties. They'll be knocking down our door to recruit us."

That caused Yunyun to brighten up immediately.

"What's more, there are going to be two different famous adventuring groups out there with us—did you know that? One of them is supposedly led by a young man with an enchanted sword, and the other—"

But I didn't get to finish my sentence.

"Aww, geez, what, you girls think you're comin' with us? Gimme a break! This ain't a field trip, y'know."

"Rex, calm down and take a closer look. These girls are from the Crimson Magic Clan, see? I'll bet they're stronger than you are."

Our new interlopers were a man and a woman. The man, whose nose had a prominent scar, towered over us, while the woman was beautiful but looked tough and had a sharp gaze. I seemed to remember that their party was…

"Whazzat? Stronger than me? These babies? What, are you jokin'? C'mon! Tell her what a stupid joke that is."

"Nah, man, I think Sophie's right. You don't know about the Crimson Magic Clan? Arch-wizards, every one of 'em, expert magic-users who all know advanced magic."

"You kiddin', Terry?! G-geez, you two, do you really know advanced magic?"

…Their party was the other famous group among us.

"No, we don't," I said, and Yunyun shook her head to underline the point.

Rex turned to his party as if to say, *See?* and gave a pointed snort.

"Huh?! That's weird, though; I was sure that's what I heard about the Crimson Magic Clan…"

"Yeah, well, sometimes rumors ain't true. Like the one about some guy with an enchanted sword who's stronger than I am. And the one

about…what'sername, the nutjob everyone says to stay clear of? Exaggerations. They gotta be… Well, whatever. You pip-squeaks wanna tag along and make some pocket money, it's your call; just make sure you stay out of our way, got it?"

With that, Rex guffawed loudly, like a little boy, and walked away with his companions.

Perhaps this was *our* baptism into this town of novices. Under other circumstances, I might have struck fear into them by beginning to chant my spell, but I was going to have to work with them on this hunt, so I didn't want to rock the boat too much…

"Megumin, don't! Calm down!"

"What?! Wh-what are you doing?! Stop that!"

As I watched Rex and his party walk away, Yunyun suddenly grabbed me from behind. She must have thought I was going to do something terrible to him.

"I am not particularly planning to do anything, so let me go! Even I am mature enough not to lose it just because some guy laughed at me. In fact, what do you think I am, some kind of outlaw?! Even more importantly, I wish you would stop pressing your chest against my back; it is very upsetting! Let me go right this instant, or I will squeeze your prided chest so hard that it will shrink down in size!"

2

Yunyun and I were back in the dim, overgrown woods, bringing up the rear of the hunting party.

"*Sniff… Sniffle… Sob…* "Beside me, Yunyun was sniffling quietly, a hand clutching her chest.

"Quiet down already! You cannot keep sniffling forever. We have to watch the rear."

"Wh-whose fault do you think this is...?! *Snf,* I thought you were going to yank them out of my body..."

About ten different groups were participating in the hunt. Each one had six to ten people. At the very head of our group was the party with the handsome guy and his magic sword. And at the very back...

"Oh-ho, fancy seein' you here! If any monsters show up, you can feel free to run and hide. Just try to keep it down, eh, kids?"

Rex was smiling broadly as his party went along, keeping a vigilant eye on our surroundings.

"Oh! S-sorry..." Yunyun shrank into herself.

Rex's party was famous in its own right, it seemed, but all its members were front-row types carrying weapons. There was Rex with his huge sword, while the others had a spear and an ax.

"It seems to me that you do not have a wizard," I said. "Did you know there are slimes in this forest? If any slimes show up—they will be impervious to your weapons, mind you—*you* may all feel free to run and hide while Yunyun here takes care of them."

"M-Megumin!" Yunyun hissed, but Rex frowned a little.

"You sure know how to talk, kid. All right, I'll take you up on that. Slimes are dangerous, that's for sure, so if we see any of them..."

And then, as if on cue, the vanguard of the hunting party started shouting.

"Monsters ahoooy!"

Rex and the others were immediately on their guard. If the notorious demon appeared, we would work to surround him, and each group's priests and wizards were to attack. If the group ahead of us had discovered the demon, then I wanted to go right to them...!

But instead I heard, "Shit, what's with this horde of small-fry monsters?! Hey, let's hurry up and kick their asses! If the forward group's found that demon, then we need to get up there…"

Rex and the other adventurers were suddenly occupied with a barrage of monsters that had appeared seemingly from nowhere.

I recognized this phenomenon. When an especially powerful monster appeared, lesser creatures ran away from it—the same thing Arnes had taken advantage of. That meant the demon had to be close.

Then I saw something drop from a tree branch toward Sophie's head. She rolled out of the way as a gloopy green thing hit the ground.

"*Lightning*!"

The slime that had tried to ambush Sophie shuddered from Yunyun's attack and was reduced to a puddle of goo.

Everyone looked up into the tree the slime had come from…!

""Heeeek?!""

There were so many Green Slimes above us that they almost seemed to be growing from the branches.

"Noooo! I can't take this anymore! I'm going back to the village!"

"Yunyun, stop crying and do something about those things! I know they are disgusting, but there are too many for me—if I tried to blow them up, I would only rain slime on us! You have to fry them with your magic!" I tried desperately to talk Yunyun down, then gave her a helpful shove.

"Stop! I get it! I'll deal with them—just quit pushing me!"

"H-hey, aren't you Crimson Magic Clan, too?! Why don't you use your magic?! You don't have to bully that girl—!" Rex exclaimed.

He was interrupted by Yunyun's shout of "*Fireball*!!" She must have been really terrified of the gloopy, gloppy slimes, because she let loose with her full power. There was a roar, and the bevy of slimes went up in flames.

"H-holy crap…!"

"I told you, didn't I?! Expert wizards, all of 'em!"

"W-way to go…!"

"Isn't she that girl, y'know, who's always playing cards by herself…?"

Rex, Terry, and everyone else in the vicinity gazed at the flaming trees in awe.

"Hmph… Not a bad job, Yunyun. You are a credit to the Crimson Magic Cl— H-hey, what are you doing?!"

"Whyyy, youuuu!" Yunyun, having successfully roasted the slimes, now turned on me.

As he and his party busily extinguished the conflagration in the trees, Rex said, "Hey, we owe you one. Sorry about earlier, makin' fun of you. Is your pint-size friend there as good as you are?"

"A-ahem, my magic is of a special kind… Consider it to be a trump card to play against a powerful foe, not the sort of thing suited for a moment like this…"

Rex raised an eyebrow at my mumblings. "…Huh, so you only *talk* about magic."

"How dare you!"

"Megumin, calm down! Back at the Guild, you said yourself that you were too mature to get upset about a little jab!"

As we scuffled, shouting came from ahead. The direction, if I was reliably informed, of the handsome sword guy. Had they finished with the monsters up there?

…Then we saw one of the adventurers from up front running our way. "This is looking bad! No way we can beat that thing! The demon showed up out of nowhere and got the drop on the guy with the sword. Now he's hurt! That thing even used advanced magic! He's gotta be at least as strong as a general of the Demon King! Everyone fall back!!"

At that, the parties in the rear, including our own group, started buzzing like a hornet's nest.

3

The group shambled through the night like a horde of undead.

"Pfeh... Enchanted sword, my ass. He got done in like a newbie on his first day. If we'd been there, we coulda hit back at that thing, am I right?"

We were on our way back to Axel. The mood of the hunting party was as dark as night, and Rex in particular was voicing his displeasure.

This person with the enchanted sword was, it seemed, quite famous indeed. The demon had attacked him the moment he had appeared. Word was that the man with the enchanted blade was known by name even among the Demon King's army.

The hero with an enchanted blade...

The hero with an enchanted blade?

I couldn't put my finger on it, but I felt like I'd heard such a thing before. A hero in waiting who wielded a blade overflowing with magical power...

Yes, that was it—I was sure I had been a student still when I first heard the tale at school...

Sophie tried to calm Rex down. "Okay, sure, but he still managed to take a swing at the thing even though the demon had wounded him. They say he cut off one of his wings. Don't you think we owe him for giving us the chance to escape? If that thing's as strong as a general of the Demon King, then I think we should just wait for the Guild to call some higher-level adventurers from another town."

Rex just spat on the ground as if he still wasn't satisfied.

*   *   *

"Welcome back, brave adventurers! We've already received a report—it sounds like this creature is a fearsome foe…!" the receptionist woman greeted us when we got back to the Guild.

It sounded like the wielder of the enchanted sword was badly hurt, while another ten or so members of the hunting party had sustained minor injuries. Such was the extent of our casualties. Priests were intoning healing magic and handing out potions, but it didn't look like we would be going in for a rematch anytime soon. The fact that our most powerful fighter had been torn to shreds the first time out wasn't very promising.

One of our adventurers shrugged. "So it goes. That thing was a high-level demon, just too much for a bunch of novices like us to handle. I say we sit down like good boys and girls while we wait for higher-level adventurers from some other town to come back us up. You've put out the word, right?"

His tone was light, but the receptionist looked distinctly uncomfortable.

…Gee, somehow I have a bad feeling about this.

"*Ahem*, everyone, I want you to listen calmly, all right? We just received information alleging that Beldia, the Dullahan general of the Demon King, has left the Demon King's castle with a massive number of undead."

At the words "general of the Demon King," a buzz ran through the Guild Hall.

"At the current time, Beldia's destination and objective are unknown. The one thing we are fairly confident about is that he won't attack this town, considering its strategic insignificance and population of novices. However…" She looked apologetic. "Until the matter of the Demon King's general is cleared up, we can't expect help from anyone else. Meaning we'll have to deal with this demon problem on our own…"

The Guild went from gloomy to completely silent.

"Don't lose hope," the receptionist said quickly. "It isn't all bad news! We've had some new adventurers register recently... One of them, believe it or not, is an Arch-priest, that all-too-rare class that specializes in exorcising demons!"

An Arch-priest. Even among advanced classes, they were unusual. They were the mortal enemies of demons and the undead, the perfect antidote to this nasty little problem.

There was just one catch...

"Jussa second. You said they registered recently... So they're, like, a Level-1 Arch-priest?"

Indeed, if they had only just registered, their level would be low, and it was unlikely they possessed many skills. As for their stats...

"No, listen to me! With only one exception, this person has incredible stats and knows every available skill—the most accomplished Arch-priest I've ever seen!"

Everyone froze. And then...

"Who is this Arch-priest?!"

"You gotta be joking! If that's the case—this demon is done...!"

"Who is it? Tell us how to find them!"

Among the babbling crowd of adventurers, a man who had been drinking until that moment stood up.

"... 'Ey, an Arch-priest like that should even be able to heal our torn-up swordsman in a hurry, right? Then he can come back and they can fight together. This one's in the bag...!"

The gathered adventurers looked at one another.

"The distinguishing features of this Arch-priest include blue hair the color of clear water and beauty befitting a goddess...!"

""""Whoo-hoooo!"""""

Almost before the receptionist finished speaking, adventurers went dashing out of the Guild.

…All of them men.

"…Looks like they're all gone," Yunyun said. "What do you think? Should we go look for her, too?"

"…They're so eager, I'm sure they'll find her before long. I must say I'm rather tired…"

"Yeah? I think I'm going to stay here awhile longer. You know, I…I think my magic actually came in handy back there, don't you? So I…"

She must have been talking about when she took out those slimes… Aha, so she was hoping one of the parties that had seen her work earlier might try to recruit her. But I just wasn't sure…

I looked around the virtually empty Guild.

"V-very well, but do not stay out too late, all right?"

"Of course! It's fine—I'll be back by morning!"

"Th-that is much too late!"

4

Adventurers were running all over town. It was evening. The laborers had finished work and were just going home for the day. And now the evening rush was compounded by rowdy adventurers hurrying every which way.

"A goddess with blue hair! Find the goddess with blue hair!"

It was a refrain that could be heard all over town, until there was a crash and the sound of a girl screaming. I guess some overeager adventurer had bumped into a bystander.

"Geez, watch where you're going! Thanks to you, I dropped my day's pay! Come on—hurry and help me pick it up! I got ten thousand eris today, and if even one eris is missing, I'll expect you to commit ritual suicide as penance!"

"L-listen, you…! How can you live with yourself?! I know you aren't— Hrrgh?!"

I looked up at the familiar voices, and indeed, it was them. The girl with blue hair was there, holding her hands over the young man's mouth.

"S-sorry 'bout that. I'll find it for you… But I don't think there's any way you really dropped ten thousand— Hold on, you've got blue hair?!"

"Hmm? What about it? Do you have a problem with my blue hair? Nobody cares what you think about it—just hurry up and find my money! Be quick about it, or I won't be in time to be first in the bath, and I worked really hard today, and I want to wash up!"

"Aww, s-sorry! …She's got the blue hair all right, but… No way she's a superpowerful Arch-priest, is she…? I thought she was supposed to be as beautiful as a goddess… Nah, can't be her. She's all muddy; no way a great cleric would get dirt under her fingernails…"

"…? What's that? Did you say something?"

"N-nah, nuthin'. Look, we're in a big hurry right now—just take this and forget about it. See ya!"

The adventurer who had bumped into the young woman gave her ten thousand eris for her trouble, then went running off.

"Whoo-hoo! Look at this! Now I'm moving up in the world! Come on—let's find the money I dropped, too! …? Hey, why are you crying?"

"…You… People really worship someone who acts like *that*…?"

"Oh, what? You should know at a glance that I'm an object of veneration."

"Like hell I should."

The young woman, still clutching her money, started to argue with the young man.

We had been told to look for a superlative Arch-priest with blue hair and looks befitting a goddess.

…Well, that girl might have had hair of similar hue, but even I could tell that wasn't her.

I dragged my exhausted body back to the inn and up to my room. Huh, I hadn't even unleashed my daily explosion yet. I would have to get Yunyun to go do it with me when she came back.

I was still thinking about that when I went to unlock the door to my room…

"Welcome home, Miss Megumin. Would you like a bath? Or me? Or perhaps you'd like to join the Axis Church?"

I closed the door again.

I tried to anyway, but it burst open with a *bam*.

"My dear, sweet Megumin, you're embarrassed! It's *so* cute! My lovely little angel!"

I was confronted by a priest I had met in the city of Arcanletia. Someone who had gotten me into a lot of trouble and gotten into a lot of trouble with me—a woman from the Axis Church.

5

"Miss…"

"You can feel free to call me Big Sis if you want."

I sat on my bed and pressed my hands to my pounding head as I addressed the woman sitting in a chair in front of me, holding Chomusuke and smiling brightly. "Miss, I have a lot of questions for you."

"Cecily—it's Cecily. It's all well and good, you referring to me as your sister, but I really think we're close enough to take the next step and start addressing each other by name."

"Miss, why are you here?"

I was sure I had locked the door when I went out that morning. So how had she gotten in? And anyway, back in Arcanletia, hadn't she been effectively committing terrorism under the guise of inviting people to join her church?

"It's *Cecily*. And… Well, if I told you the whole story, it would take forever…" She put a finger to her lips in thought. "What a pain to explain. Let's just call it Lady Aqua's guidance."

"Let's not! For one thing, I want to know how you got in here when I locked the door!"

Cecily looked very serious at that. "As a matter of fact… Megumin, I came here because I have a request for you."

"You can't throw me off just by looking all serious."

This was Cecily's story in a few words: Zesta, the highest official of the Axis Church, had allegedly heard the voice of the goddess Aqua. Cecily insisted that this was possible—Zesta might be pathetic, but he was also one of the top Arch-priests in the Axis Church, and he possessed the ability to receive prophecies from his goddess.

"Fair enough. I mean, I took him for a simple deviant, but he was powerful enough to intimidate even Arnes. Prophecies, huh? That's surprisingly…" …*priestly*, I thought, once more revisiting my opinion of him. "So what did this prophecy say? Is catastrophe coming to Axel? Or perhaps, has the hero who will defeat the Demon King been born?!"

"Lord Zesta did mention this town. He said Lady Aqua was broadcasting holy waves from somewhere in Axel. He claims the voice said, *I am Aqua. Yes, the goddess Aqua, the very deity worshipped by the Axis Church! If you be my follower…! …It would really be a big help if you could lend me some money!*"

"This prophecy is beginning to sound like a confidence job."

It was strange enough to be receiving a "broadcast," but then it turned out to be requesting money from the Axis followers?

"We weren't sure what the transmission was supposed to mean, but the one thing that was clear was that Lady Aqua is truly in trouble. If there's one thing I can vouch for, it's that Lord Zesta would never invoke our lady's name for personal gain... I don't know why Lady Aqua needs money, but I, the beautiful Axis priestess, have been dispatched to this place to discover the reason!"

"I see the Axis Church still has plenty of time to kill."

The whole beautiful-priestess schtick was too much trouble to even comment on. Anyway, I didn't see how this mysterious prophecy and I were even connected.

"Now that I'm here, I understand the meaning of Lady Aqua's message. This town is in the grip of a demon, the great enemy of the Axis Church." Still holding Chomusuke and still looking grim, Cecily came over so she was beside me where I sat on the bed.

"It's true that there's a demon in the woods who has been causing no end of trouble for the adventurers around here... You think that's what your prophecy was referring to?"

Still looking very serious, Cecily wormed her way under my sheets.

...She seemed to be able to do anything with a stern face.

"Yes, and one of the ironclad precepts of the Axis faith is 'Thou shalt kill demons.' Lady Aqua wants money in this town. Lord Zesta claims something is going to happen here. Put those two facts together and... Yes!" Now she had established herself so firmly between my sheets that only her head poked out. "I'm to take the money entrusted to me by the Church, hire some people, and kill the demon in this town—that's the meaning of the prophecy!"

"A-are you sure about that...? And incidentally, could you get out of there? This is my room, and that's my bed..."

Cecily ignored me, happily burying her face in the sheets and taking a deep sniff.

...*Hey.*

"The first thing I thought of when I got into town was you and all you had done for us, Megumin..."

"Excuse me, but I do not care, and I would very much appreciate it if you got out of my bed." I tried to pull the sheets off her, but Cecily resisted me fiercely and with surprising strength. She was indeed a pretty person—when her mouth was shut. Why did Axis followers always turn out to be such good-for-nothings?!

"But there are hardly any Axis followers in this town. Not even enough to run a proper church—so there's no one I can ask for help! And that's why I came to you, Megumin!"

"Absolutely not—count me out! I want nothing more to do with you all! And stop smelling my pillow!"

Deprived of the sheets, which I had finally wrenched away from her, Cecily rolled over in my bed and produced a pouch from her bag. "Five million if you help me find the Arch-priest rumored to be staying in this town. And once we defeat the demon, ten million."

"Done."

And so I found myself once more joining forces with the Axis Church.

6

Cecily and I were walking around town.

"Hey, how's it going? Did you find her?!"

"You mean the incredibly talented, unbelievably beautiful Arch-priest with blue hair? Ain't seen her! I did see a drunken street performer with blue hair! Dammit, where is this beautiful Arch-priest we keep looking for…?!"

Apparently, the hunt was ongoing; adventurers continued to swarm everywhere.

"It looks like all their searching hasn't gotten them anywhere. You really think we're going to be the ones to find her?" I said.

"Where do they think they're looking?" Cecily said. "I think they ought to try somewhere new. Megumin, when I say *Arch-priest*, what kind of place comes to mind?"

"Places an Arch-priest might be… Hmm… Maybe praying in church or holding services at the communal graveyard to soothe wandering spirits…?"

We were, allegedly, looking for an exceptionally talented Arch-priest. Someone like that must have great, purehearted faith…

"As a priest of the Axis Church, let me tell you what *I* would be doing about this time of day… For one thing, I'd be rushing to the public bath in order to be the first one in. Then I would grab a nice, cold Crimson Neroid with a side of fried frog, pick a fight with the drunk eyeballing my luscious body, and then finally I would throw some rocks at an Eris church before I went home, full and satisfied."

"And you call yourself a cleric?"

Was there really a chance that this Arch-priest was a member of the Axis Church, just like the woman beside me? No, the receptionist had said our quarry had tremendous stats, not to mention she was as beautiful as a goddess. That would seem to make it exceedingly unlikely that she was an Axis follower.

…Unlikely but not impossible.

"*Ahem*… My intuition is never wrong. If we go to the places I just mentioned, I'm sure we'll run into that Arch-priest. So let's go, okay? The baths should be empty right about now…"

"You sure it's not just because you want a bath? Come on—let's try going to the church first or something."

"Ahhh… Megumin, the search can wait till tomorrow—come take a bath with your dear big sis, okay?! We can wash each other's backs!"

"If you aren't actually interested in looking for this woman, then I'm going home!"

The first place I headed was the Eris church, but I promptly regretted bringing Cecily there.

"C'mon—open up! I know you've got an Arch-priest in there who can slay that demon! If you don't want me to break this door down, then let me in!!" Cecily was busily pounding away on the door.

The agonized shouting of an Eris priestess could be heard from within. "No, we don't! And I'm afraid Axis followers and anyone else associated with their Church are forbidden from entering this building! Go away! Go away, I tell you!!"

Cecily tsked and looked at the implacable door. "Megumin, you're up. I know you can do this. Use your magic to blow this church to bits."

"I can't do that! …You could have just talked to them like a normal person—why did you have to start by pounding on their door? The more trouble you cause, the worse things get for us, so just stop." I sighed and stood in front of the door. "Um. I'm an adventurer; maybe we could talk?"

"Are you also looking for this Arch-priest? I'm afraid you'll just have to go home; there are no gorgeous Arch-priests here! I swear, every adventurer in the city has come by here…!"

…I guess we were all thinking the same thing.

"I apologize for the ruckus," I said. "It so happens that a very powerful demon has appeared near this town, and we were hoping to enlist the aid of this Arch-priest in eliminating him..." There was silence from the other side of the door, which I took as a sign that they were listening to me. "We pinned our hopes on a powerful adventurer, but he was wounded. We need someone to help us heal him and go after that demon, but..."

Then, at last, the door of the church opened just a crack.

"...I'm afraid there's no one like that in this church."

A woman, who I assumed was a priestess, peeked out, looking worn. I bowed and was about to turn and go when she said, "She's not in this church, but...there's an orphanage nearby where they're doing food distribution for the needy. I don't know for sure she's there, but itinerant priests frequently stop to do good works at places like that." Then the priestess smiled at me.

"...! Thank you very m—"

I was interrupted by a *chak* sound from within the church, followed by a scream. I tried to get a glance at what was inside...

"*Strike!*"

Cecily declared, looking very satisfied about the window she had broken with the stone she'd picked up off the ground.

We were on our way to the orphanage.

"Are you stupid?! Why is every single follower of the Axis Church a complete, inveterate moron?! *Strike*, my foot—I know you don't have the best relations with the Eris Church, but where was the call to go that far?!"

"It's all very strange, I admit. I've been just bubbling ever since I got to this town. It's like I'm in even better form than usual. Maybe it's a gift from the great Lady Aqua?"

"If that 'form' is a blessing from your deity, then when I meet Aqua at the end of my life, I swear I'm going to sock her."

"Phew… That was a close one, though. I can't believe such a sedate-looking priestess would have it in her to strike back…"

"Of course she would! What do you hope to gain, making even the nicest people upset?! When that friendly priestess finally snapped, I can't tell you how scared I was!"

Evening was coming along; it was already getting dark outside. The bars and restaurants we passed were noisy with people having dinner. We went to a bar with some particularly loud shouting coming from inside. Cecily seemed drawn to it like a moth to a flame…

"J-just a second—where do you think you're going?! We don't have time to play around; we have to get to that orphanage before the evening distribution ends!"

"Yes, but they just sound like they're having so much fun in there…! My Axis intuition is telling me our Arch-priest is right in there…!"

"What would someone like that be doing in a place like this?! Traveling performers drink in this bar, not purehearted and unbelievably amazing clerics!"

"Aww, but—but—Lord Zesta, one of the most unbelievably amazing clerics in our entire religion, goes to an even worse tavern every few days…"

"Don't besmirch the good name of the clergy by acting like he's one of them!"

Cecily finally gave in, and I dragged her away toward the orphanage.

When we arrived at the orphanage that was distributing the food, however…

"Mmf… I thee, tho she didn'f come here, either… *(Gulp!)* Seconds, please, an extra-large scoop!!" Looking very serious, Cecily demanded seconds of the food she was stuffing her face with—food that was supposed to be going to the needy. I knew she talked about doing whatever you wanted, but really. Were all Axis followers this way?

"No, I'm afraid no one matching that description has ever come to help serve. But hair the color of water, my goodness… There *is* someone with blue hair who comes to *get* food here all the time… Could that be the person you're looking for…?"

I highly doubted a beautiful, capable Arch-priest would stoop to scamming the dole. Which made this another dead end.

Cecily thanked the woman doing the distribution, then, patting her bulging belly, said, "Hoo… Best meal I ever served myself. Megumin, I'm sort of sleepy now that my stomach's full. I'm sure our Arch-priest is getting some nice shut-eye right about now. How about we go back to the inn and call it a night?"

C-curse her…!

The only other place left to search was the communal graveyard. It was perfectly dark by this time, and the graveyard, located on a hillside outside of town, had an uncanny atmosphere. With nothing but a lantern for light, Cecily and I stood smack in the middle of the cemetery, but there didn't seem to be anyone else in the whole place. I knew it had been my suggestion, but I was starting to doubt whether an Arch-priest would really come to a place like this.

"Eeeeek!" Cecily screamed, and startled, I exclaimed, "Bwaaaah?!" I almost dropped the lantern but caught myself and looked quickly around. "Wh-what is it? What's wrong?! Did an undead appear?!" I hid behind Cecily and looked around like my life depended on it…!

"Hee-hee, pfffft! Megumin, you went 'bwaaaah'! 'Bwaaaah,' she says! My goodness, it's just the cutest little eeeyow-ow-ow! I'm sorry—I was just making a little joke; I won't do it again, so stop that! Forgive me!"

Just as I was smacking Cecily with my staff, Chomusuke, who had stuck close to me ever since we left town, looked up to the sky and froze.

She was looking just behind Cecily and me. Staring, not moving a muscle…

"…Miss. Um, you're a priest, right? I have something to ask of you."

"G-go ahead. I warn you, though, I only know simple healing magic. I haven't practiced Turn Undead enough to use it, and I don't remember the incantation anyway, all right?"

Geez, some priest.

…In the moonlight, I saw a shadow, and it wasn't from the lantern. It shifted and squirmed like fox fire…

"…Will you turn around on my count?"

"…Okay. We'll turn around at the same time, and whatever's there, we'll fight it together. Sound good?"

"Understood—here I go, then."

I took a breath.

At the same moment, there was a scrape of something stepping on the earth behind us.

""One… Two…Three…!""

We shouted, then dashed away without turning around.

"Hey, Megumin, this wasn't our agreement!"

"Look who's talking! It's your job as a cleric to stay behind so a young girl can escape!"

We argued as we ran along, never looking back, straight toward town!

"But I'm basically your employer!"

"I haven't received any payment, and anyway, the quest was to find someone, not to be a bodyguard!"

Then we heard it.

"U-um…"

Or anyway, it seemed we did: a frail, lonely voice calling to us as we fled.

"Y-you're awful… *Hff, hff…!* When did you get so cynical, Megumin? You used to be so sweet and gullible!"

"I learned my lesson after taking enough licks from you guys!" When we had finally reached the town gate, we stood there, out of breath and dripping sweat. "By the way, I thought I heard a woman's voice when we ran off… Do you think it was the Arch-priest we were looking for?"

Cecily, fanning her sweaty face with her hand, said, "No, it wasn't. I glanced back just before we got out of the cemetery. There was a pretty girl standing there in the moonlight, with wavy hair and a face as pale as an undead…!"

"Ugh, no more! I don't want to hear any more!"

7

It was the day after Cecily and my lengthy but fruitless search. I found Yunyun, who had apparently waited at the Guild all night, slumped over a table, sniffling.

"*Sniff… Sniff…* I didn't know what else to do…! I kept thinking if I just waited another hour, someone might come back who had seen what I did and want to talk to me, so I kept telling myself: just a little longer, just a little longer…!"

"And that's how you ended up not going home at all last night? You are the most pathetic!"

After the adventurers had gone rushing out of the Guild, it seemed they had dispersed without ever coming back. As for Cecily, who had been so riled up yesterday, she was lounging at the inn today.

I had woken her up—she was staying in the same building—and she said she was going to catch a few winks and immediately went back to sleep, claiming that she had been up all night worrying about how I had been hardened by the tribulations of life.

She could try to pin this on me, but I knew it was because she had been up drinking at the bar at our inn until late last night.

Axis followers certainly did love their freedom. Did they have any concept at all of structures or rules? In any event, having officially accepted her request, I couldn't afford to just kill time. Unfortunately, as far as what to do about the demon, at the moment, it seemed like my only real options were to wait for the adventurer with the enchanted sword to heal up or to find that Arch-priest.

…I was as lost as the sulky Yunyun, who still had her face planted on the table.

"Yo, if it isn't the all-talk wizard. Not going out to look for the notorious Arch-priest?"

Who should appear but Rex, a stein of beer in his hand despite the fact that it was still morning.

"Oh," I said, "if it isn't our very functional adventurer friend, the one who went running off with this all-talk wizard the moment we heard our swordsman got done in! What's the matter with you? Has your crippling fear of the demon driven you to drink first thing in the morning?"

"H-huh…?! You've got big nerve for such a little girl!"

"Excuse me, but I would like to know what exactly you mean by *little*. Depending on your answer, I may ask you to step outside!"

"Gosh, Megumin, can't you even go one minute without getting into a fight with him? I'm sorry—she's been in a bad mood since yesterday…!"

Yunyun tried to cover for me, but Rex frowned. "Aww, it's… Look, I'm sorry. I'm not feeling my best, either. I didn't see hide or hair of that Arch-priest everyone's looking for. I shouldn't have let myself get sucked into that. Sorry."

He was supposed to be some big-name adventurer, and he couldn't find the Arch-priest? For that matter, an entire Guild's worth of adventurers conducting a town-wide manhunt couldn't find her, either? Maybe our Arch-priest had already moved on to another city.

"Anyway, hey. I didn't come here *just* to pick a fight with you. I've got some business… Truth is, I have some juicy info on that demon. I don't know how good you really are, but I saw how powerful your friend was yesterday… How about it? You interested?"

Then Rex grinned at us.

A certain monster had been sighted at the foot of a mountain some ways from town. That, it seemed, was Rex's "juicy info."

"Tell us already. What was this 'certain monster'?"

"Heh-heh, one that's pretty dangerous for novices. I'll understand if you want to pull out, 'kay? I think the three of us can manage by ourselves."

Yunyun and I had joined Rex's party and headed for the mountain in question. The man called Terry had the reins of a horse he was leading, which was pulling a gigantic cage.

"Here's a hint: This thing is black and huge," Sophie said. "You should know what that means—after all, you were the ones who told the Guild, right? About how that demon was looking for a big, black magical beast?"

I felt my blood run cold. Yunyun had stopped dead in her tracks. Based on her facial expression, I could see we were on the same page.

"Excuse me. This monster we're about to go looking for, could it be…?"

"Oh-ho, caught on, have ya? That's right—it's a Beginner's Bane."

Yunyun and I did an about-face and started heading back the way we had come.

The Beginner's Bane. It was called that for a reason—and *we* were beginners.

"H-hey, I thought you Crimson Magic Clansfolk were all supposed to be expert wizards! I know I joked about you going home, but I didn't expect you to actually do it!"

"It's precisely *because* we are expert wizards! Beginner's Banes are clever and wary, not to mention extremely fast. They're smart enough that sometimes they even set ambushes, and they know to attack the weakest-looking members of a group first. That means poor, defenseless wizards are often the first thing on the menu."

"Their speed also means they can close in on you in an instant, so being in the rear guard doesn't help much. And our levels are still pretty low…"

For all those reasons, Beginner's Banes were dangerous not just to beginners but to wizards in general. Considering that we were both low-level wizards, we would almost certainly be its first target.

"C'mon—you'll be fine. We've hunted lots of Banes in our time. We just want you to use a little magic on it when we capture it. We'll take care of you—I promise."

Rex sounded relaxed, but I doubted whether someone with more muscle than brains like him was really equipped to evade a Bane's surprise attack…

"…Um. So you just want me to use Sleep on it so you can capture it? But what are you going to do with this Beginner's Bane once you have it?"

Rex jabbed a thumb at the steel cage the horse was dragging. "It's obvious, ain't it? We put the Bane in the cage, then take the cage back to town. That demon is looking for a big, black magical beast. It's not a coincidence a Bane shows up at the exact same time. It's gotta be the one he's looking for, right? Maybe like his pet or something?"

So they planned to use the Beginner's Bane as bait to draw out the demon.

"We ice the fiend or we chase him outa that forest. Either way, the Guild gives us the reward, and we split it fifty-fifty. What do you say? Not bad, eh?"

Rex gave us a pointed smile.

8

Beginner's Banes often concealed themselves near groups of minor monsters like goblins or kobolds, monsters that would be attractive hunting targets to inexperienced adventurers. When the newbies came for the small fries, the Bane would have its next meal.

In other words, if you wanted to hunt a Beginner's Bane...!

"Blade of Wind!"

"Whoo-hoo! Look at that power—that's the Crimson Magic Clan for you! All right, in we go!" Rex, wielding his great, two-handed broadsword, charged into the center of the goblin horde. Sophie followed him with her spear, leaving Terry with his ax to protect Yunyun and me.

It turned out that the stories of them being a famous, highly effective party were more than just talk. Rex took out dozens of goblins in the blink of an eye, then looked around vigilantly. Beginner's Banes generally tried to protect the goblins or other creatures that served as their bait. If the creature was nearby, then our attack on its goblins should...

"Terry, behind you!" Rex shouted—and at the same moment, there was a great shaking of the bushes behind us, and a black shadow came leaping out! It was heading straight for Yunyun, but Terry stepped between them.

"Grrrrrr!"

"C-come and get me, you overgrown house pet!" Terry was buying us some time against the Bane, but Yunyun had to chant her spell, and quick...!

"*Sleep!*" She pointed her wand at the Beginner's Bane, and the massive black creature slumped to the ground without so much as a yelp.

""""Whoa!"""""

Rex and the others, who promptly moved to capture the beast, were suitably impressed. They surrounded the now motionless Bane.

"You said your name was Yunyun, right? You sure know how to handle yourself! Any chance you're interested in joining our party?"

"Yeah, there aren't too many wizards with power like yours. What do you say? I'm here, so you won't be the only woman around. I think it could be nice, don't you?"

"We're all muscle-brained frontline fighters—it would really help us to get a wizard in here!"

"What?! Y-you want me?!" Yunyun, totally overwhelmed by the chorus of praise, blushed and stood petrified.

She had been so eager to be invited to a group, but when the moment finally came, she choked. Yunyun looked at me helplessly, but I figured this was part of her "training." I decided to let her fend for herself.

"Ahhh, we can sit down and talk about it when we get back to town. First we'd better take care of this thing."

"You're right. You think that demon will come to negotiate with us when he sees us heading back to town with this thing in a cage? High-level demons are supposed to be intelligent, and I hear this one knows how to talk. You said you had a conversation with him, right, Megumin?"

"Yes, well. I must say, looking back on it, he seemed rather friendly, as demons go. But…"

They completed the capture of the Beginner's Bane. All that was left was to drag it back to town and wait for the demon to show up.

"What's the matter? Something on your mind? …Hey, come to think of it, you've still been all talk on this quest, just like last time. Is it just me, or have you not done anything to help out around here?" Rex was teasing but looked at me dubiously. I instantly felt as if a vein might burst in my forehead, but I knew that my short temper and eagerness to pick a fight were bad habits.

There was indeed something else on my mind at that moment. We were dealing with a high-level demon, even if we did just have his pet hostage, and I wondered if things would really go as smoothly as we hoped.

…In a word, something had felt off this entire time. Perhaps this black magical beast wasn't a Beginner's Bane at all…

"Well, whatever. Let's haul this thing back to town and at least celebrate capturing it."

Rex seemed oblivious to my unease—and that's when it happened.

"*There* you are!!"

Rex's suggestion was drowned out by a voice so loud, it seemed to come from everywhere at once.

9

For a second, I couldn't tell where the voice had come from or what had happened. All of us instinctively froze, and then he appeared.

"You little stinkers! What do you think you're doing to Lady Wolbach—? Ohhhh, you'll pay!!"

His body was massive, such a polished black that it reflected light. I was pretty sure he'd had two giant, bat-like wings before, but now he had only one. He still had the twisted, cruel horns and fangs, though. There was no mistaking it: He was our high-level demon, the one I had met in the woods.

And he was charging out of the trees right at us, enraged!

"Whoa?! H-hey, this here's a Beginner's B— Argh?!"

"Agh!!"

"Guh?!"

The three adventurers surrounding the Bane's cage were sent flying before they could draw their weapons. In fact, Yunyun and I, not being experienced in close combat, could hardly even tell what had happened to them. Each of them was collapsed in a different place, some ways away on the ground, and none of them showed any sign of moving. The demon, indeed, crouched down near the Beginner's Bane.

"Lady Wolbach! Open your eyes, Lady Wolbach!!"

The name he was desperately calling sounded somehow familiar. Wait...*Wolbach*?

"Uh, Megumin, aren't we in kind of a tight spot here? What do you think—will he let us run away again…?"

There was an instant when I thought I might remember why the name seemed so important, but I was interrupted by Yunyun tugging on my sleeve and trembling.

"Shh," I said, "let's not act hastily—we'll edge our way out of here slowly so that we don't give him an opportunity to attack." As I spoke, I began to back away from the demon, who was still shouting at the Beginner's Bane.

Then, suddenly, the demon cocked his head in surprise. It was an unsettlingly innocent gesture from such a vile-looking creature.

"'Ey... 'Ey, 'ey, 'ey, 'ey. This thing's just a Beginner's Bane. The hell's going on here?"

The demon got to his feet, mumbling something, then turned his gaze, eyes as blank as glass orbs, on us.

""?!""

When our eyes met, I experienced a fear unlike any I had ever known. This guy was bad news—the worst news. He was vastly more powerful than Arnes, the last high-level demon I'd fought.

And suddenly, I connected the dots.

"Hey, you over there. What's the deal with this thing? I caught Lady Wolbach's scent—I'd know it anywhere—and hauled myself all the way out here... I mean, damn, from a distance it even *looks* like her."

Wolbach was the name Arnes had used...

"Hey, what's with this? Why do you smell like Lady Wolbach? You friends of hers?"

Yunyun and I tried to back up as the demon crossed his arms and thought.

...No question now. The thing this demon was after was my familiar, Chomusuke.

Unfortunately, there was no time to be (justifiably) proud of my familiar for being the target of such a powerful demon. We had to get out of here somehow...! My staff was still in my hands, and I started to chant a spell under my breath.

With speed belying his size, the demon leaped in close to me. He took a sniff of my clothes. "...Hmm, you smell like her most of all. Fresh scent, too—no later than this morning, I'd say." Having that awful face so close to me made me desperate to scramble away. But he was too close now; resistance was futile. As the monster sniffed at me, I remembered that Chomusuke had indeed cuddled up to me that morning.

I would have to strangle the little fur ball when I got home.

"Hey, say somethin', kid. You know, I think I've met you before. You're the Crimson Magic Clan kid I ran into in the woods, aren't you?"

I nodded, emphatically but silently. The demon nodded back, evidently satisfied.

"Huh, I see… The seal was in Crimson Magic Village. And you guys are Crimson Magic Clansfolk. Hey, it makes sense now. It finally makes sense!"

I didn't know what "made sense," but I felt like I would cry if that face got any closer, so I wished he would back off. In fact, beside me, Yunyun's eyes were already brimming with tears.

"Right, kids! If you're Crimson Magic Clansfolk, you oughta know something about where Lady Wolbach is. Don't pretend you don't; you obviously saw her this morning."

Murderous intent was rolling off the demon now, and I started to fear for my life.

"Wh-why do you and your ilk insist on referring to my Chomusuke by this bizarre name, *Wolbach*? I can guarantee you have the wrong cat. If you like, I can find you a nice, cute kitten instead, so just leave Chomusuke alone!"

"Ch-Chomusuke? Whazzat? Hang on, I think I've heard that name somewhere. Where *was* it? …Aw yeah, it was that pip-squeak…!"

I couldn't imagine what he meant by that. Yunyun and I stood paralyzed as the demon shook his head back and forth vigorously, as if he was trying to control something that had welled up within him.

"I don't want to have to go at it with you Crimson Magic kids if I don't have to… I think the pip-squeak'd come after me anyway… So listen up, okay? I need. Lady Wolbach—bring me Lady Wolbach. If you really don't know who she is, just bring me everyone you saw this morning. Got that? This is a…what's the word…? Oh yeah, a trade. You bring me Lady Wolbach, and you don't get hurt. Oh, and I spare your little town, too."

"We're supposed to take a demon at his word?!" Yunyun, who had been too petrified to speak until that moment, finally realized he was talking about Chomusuke and gripped her wand fiercely.

"Hey, cool your jets. Us demons never break a contract once it's made. That's, like, our number one, absolute law. Besides, I think my great, bad self is bein' pretty friendly, don't you? Okay, so I roughed up the kid with the enchanted sword a bit. But what else was I supposed to do? He's a wanted man among us demons."

I restrained Yunyun with a hand on her shoulder—she looked like she might launch a spell at any moment—and said, "A wanted man? This famous wielder of the enchanted blade who's in Axel right now—he's wanted among the demons?"

The monster responded, "Aww yeah, I forgot. I ain't properly introduced myself. My name is Host. High-level demon and right hand of the Dark God Lady Wolbach. Enchanted-sword wielders could take down a god if they felt like it—you can't be too careful around 'em."

10

"Are we really going to negotiate with that monster?" asked Yunyun as she led the horse by the reins.

"…I'm not sure yet. But if we can fix all this just by giving him that fur ball, it might be worth it."

After all, we weren't just dealing with a major demon here but an accessory to a Dark God. If we weren't careful, things could turn out even worse for us than for the guy with the enchanted sword.

Yunyun went silent when she heard my answer.

Rex and the others were sleeping peacefully in the cage formerly occupied by the Beginner's Bane. The two of us could hardly hope to get them back to town by ourselves, so we turned the cage into a make-shift carriage. The three of them showed no sign of opening their eyes yet.

They were a group of hearty adventurers, and they had been simply dismissed in the blink of an eye. And now, allegedly, if we gave Chomusuke to their attacker, neither we nor the town would come to harm. The obvious implication being that if we *didn't* give Chomusuke to the demon, not only we, but many innocent townspeople, would suffer as a result.

I wasn't exactly holding out hope that someone would conveniently come along and rescue us, as had happened in Crimson Magic Village and Arcanletia. Rex and his party were down for the count, and if there was anyone else in Axel who could go toe to toe with a demon, I didn't know about them…

The wheels on the cage clattered along. Right about the time we were reaching the town gate, Yunyun, who had been deep in thought, said, "Listen, Megumin, I think we can just ignore whatever that demon says. He's a *demon*; we don't even know if he'll keep his so-called promise. And I know this town is supposed to be full of novices, but there are lots of good, experienced adventurers here. So we just…"

It was an unusual thing to hear from Yunyun, who was generally so naively trusting, eager to do the right thing, and eager to help people even when she was the one who inevitably got burned. Maybe experience really had taught her a thing or two.

Never mind whether or not they were *good* things.

She was beginning to learn to make her way in the world, but I was a little worried that she might start hanging around the wrong crowd…

I didn't answer as we passed through the gate. I looked to one side, where I saw those two people again, swinging pickaxes and looking like they were having a nice time as always. If I shirked my duty now, these two—unreliable as they appeared, yet fun-loving—would be among the first to pay the price, just outside the town gates as they were.

I clutched my staff and felt the power well up within me.

Lonely Girl Awakening

Yesterday, something unprecedented happened: Somebody was turned down for admittance into the Axis Church. Me.

My old self might have been completely broken by it, but today I was sitting in the corner of the Adventurers Guild that had practically become my personal seat...

"...So what you're saying is, I can't try to solve the entire problem at once; I have to figure out what's behind it and deal with the root causes one by one?"

"That's exactly what I'm saying, my disciple. As they say, haste makes waste—you'll have more luck if you take your time dealing with things."

I was receiving lessons from a man who described himself as a guru.

"But, mister, I don't know what the causes *are*..."

I was feeling pretty low, but my teacher smiled gently. "Trust me—we'll figure it out together. Don't worry—all will be well... Ah, but I've dried out my throat with too much talking; would it be all right if I ordered a beer?"

"Of course!"

He ordered his drink and downed it in a single gulp—he made it look pretty tasty.

"Ahhh, that's good! Now, what were we talking about? Oh, that's right, your inability to make friends."

"Yes—I just can't bring myself to talk to strangers... How can I learn to talk to anyone I want to, like you?!" He was famous in this Guild for being acquainted with just about everyone.

"I get my vigor from the alcohol here. Alcohol is the best. Alcohol soaks your life in pleasure, my disciple. Mind if I order another round?"

"Go ahead! Mister, I think I'm too young to drink... Isn't there anything else I can do?"

He ordered another beer—I had lost count of how many this was—and drank it down. "Anything else? All right, well, just you wait. I'm sure by the time I finish drinking this, I'll have had a flash of inspiration."

"Please, sir, have another!"

An hour later...

"I can't drink another drop..."

"Mister, please tell me! How can I make friends and meet people?" I shook my increasingly lethargic instructor violently, but he remained splayed out on the table.

"I'm afraid this old man just doesn't... Wait, I've got it! You seem like a well-developed young lady; maybe if you wore something that showed a little more cleavage..." I twitched as the old man stared up at me. "N-n-no, that was just a joke, a joke! You're so serious all the time—I just wanted to make sure you were really listening...! And the part where I said I would give you some life lessons if you just treated me to a drink—that was a joke, too! I'll cover everything, your drinks included, of course!"

"I don't care about any of that!" I pounded the table.

"Heeek! I-I'm sorry! I never thought you would get so angry—with the red eyes! I got carried away! I'm sorry!"

But none of that was what I wanted to hear!

"I said, none of that matters! Mister, hurry up and tell me how I can make friends and find party members! I'm begging you, I'm at my wits' end—you're my only hope!!"

"A-a-and I wish I could help you; I do!"

My eyes were probably burning red because of my heightened emotions, but I couldn't be concerned about that right now. I had finally found someone to give me some advice, and I wasn't going to let him get away!

"O-over there...on the bulletin board..."

"Yes, the bulletin board?!"

He said in a meek voice, "On the board, maybe you could p-post something about being willing to p-pay someone to be f-frie— No, no, I'm just joking. Of course I'm not seriously suggesting that!"

Before he could even squeak out that thought, I had yanked his shirt collar, causing him to get all teary.

"Thank you, sir. That's a fantastic idea! I'll try it!!"

"You will?"

For a man who had come up with a superb suggestion, he sounded awfully surprised.

The Explosion Girl of Axel

1

Fortunately, Rex and the others were okay despite having been attacked by Host. Yunyun and I dropped them off at the Eris church and headed for the Adventurers Guild.

Now, then.

"Megumin, listen, okay? Demons, you know, they're very smart and very sneaky—they're the last ones you should trust. You've heard the story, right? The one about the demon who claims he'll grant you three wishes in exchange for your soul! Do you know how many wizards have taken him up on it—just to find out they don't get any wishes at all, and he just takes their soul?!"

My mind, though, was made up.

"I'm telling you, making deals with demons doesn't get you anywhere. You can give him Chomusuke, but I'm sure he'll just do whatever he wants...!"

Specifically, made up about what to do...

"I guess you might like a demon, eh, Megumin? He'd growl, 'I'll give you the powers of darkness…' and you'd swallow it hook, line, and sinker!"

…to this jabbering, endlessly lecturing, yet completely naive girl!

I turned abruptly to Yunyun. "You are one to talk, considering how you'll go running off after anyone who says anything even remotely nice about you! You might recall that I was the preeminent student in Crimson Magic Village! I don't need the loneliest girl in the Clan's history to remind me about old stories!"

"Th-the loneliest girl…!!"

I managed to peel Yunyun off me before she could strangle me and held out my hand in a conciliatory gesture. "Now, just wait a moment—I think there's been a big misunderstanding! All right, so maybe 'the loneliest girl in the Clan's history' was going a bit too far. I'm aware you've made all sorts of friends since we got to Axel, like that weird old guy and the dude who spends all day trying to pick up younger girls. Allow me to promote you to 'most gullible girl in the Clan's history.'"

"…I think 'lonely' was better…" Remembering her own situation, Yunyun put her hands to her face and sniffled audibly.

"Look, let's talk," I said. "And perhaps in due course, we will be able to do something about the friends you make. I'm afraid if I leave you to your own devices, you really will fall in with the wrong crowd at this rate." I ushered Yunyun, who was still sniffling, toward the door of the Guild.

"…And so Rex and his party were also handily defeated by the demon…"

""""What're we gonna dooooo?!""""

The collective staff of the Guild sent up a wail at our report; I simply dragged Yunyun over to a corner table. We proceeded to hold a strategy meeting.

"As you can see, we can no longer turn to the Guild for help. First, let's take stock of the situation."

"The situation… Well, the two most powerful groups in town both got sent packing, and we can't find this Arch-priest who'll supposedly solve our problem. A Dullahan general of the Demon King is on the move, and other towns are too busy with him to send us help. And that demon…Host… Was that what he said his name was? Come to think of it, he never set a time limit on our negotiations. I can't imagine he'll wait forever to get that cat."

Yunyun was looking very dispirited. With no hope of reinforcements from other towns, we could hardly expect things to get any better. And she was right; no one had ever located that Arch-priest. Meaning…

"Meaning our only hope really is to give Chomusuke to that monster… But that's the one thing I *refuse* to do! I've grown pretty fond of her myself; I'm not just going to give her up!"

She angrily grabbed Chomusuke off the table where she was resting, prompting a puzzled look from me.

"…I really do think you have been laboring under some kind of misunderstanding. I haven't said a thing about negotiating with him," I told her.

"What?! B-but on our way home, you looked so deep in thought… Wait, don't tell me…"

"Would *I*, of all people, be intimidated into negotiating with anyone? A member of the Crimson Magic Clan never backs down from a fight. I've decided. I've decided…that I'm going to defeat that demon!"

"That guy with the enchanted sword couldn't do it! Rex and his whole party couldn't do it! And when we first saw that demon, you were terrified! I know you aren't a *complete* idiot, Megumin, so you must understand that he is much more powerful than you!"

"Your words pierce me like thorns! Yes, I could tell how powerful that demon was just by looking at him. Far more powerful even than Arnes, I would wager. But I have a way of defeating him. Seeing as our Arch-priest is proving elusive, the only one in this town who can stand up to him is me, is it not?"

Yunyun just clenched her fists and went silent. Then she jumped to her feet and slammed her fists on the table...!

"Fine, just...do whatever you want! Megumin, you're the stupide—Gah?!"

She was about to run off somewhere, but I grabbed the hem of her cape and held her fast. When she looked back at me, her eyes were full of tears and she was coughing, but I had a bright smile on my face. "We're friends, are we not?"

"You want me to *help* you?! You want to get *me* involved in this?! We're not friends; we're rivals! If you think I'll do whatever you want just because you use the word *friends*, you've got another thing coming, all right?! I hate the fact that I'm a little happy right now!!"

2

I brought Yunyun, still puffy-faced, to a certain place.

"I am no fool, Yunyun. I have no intention of challenging that thing to a fair fight. Ergo, the first thing we need is a war chest."

"'War chest'...? But this is the place where we sleep..."

Yes, we were at our inn.

"Things are going to get a little dangerous now, so you shouldn't come any farther, Yunyun. Just hang out over there and kill some time."

"Huh...? Okay, but 'dangerous'...? Wait, Megumin, how exactly are you planning to get this 'war chest'?"

"I think it would be better for both of us if you didn't ask. Okay, see you later!"

"J-just a second! Seriously, what are you…?!"

I could hear (but ignored) Yunyun behind me as I mounted the stairs and headed for one particular room.

I stood before the door and took a deep breath. Then, my resolve set, I knocked twice and heard a familiar voice from inside.

"Yes? Come in."

I opened the door, and there she was, splayed out on the bed, munching on some kind of snack: Cecily. As I stepped into the room, I joined my hands, adopting a pose of supplication—or prayer, if you will.

"Big Sis Cecily, could you gimme my allowance?"

"How much do you need? Just tell your big sister! What do you want to buy? A house? Would you like to get a new home with your big sis? Don't worry—with your sister's good looks, we'll rope in some rich adventurer in no time!"

I somehow managed to restrain Cecily before she rushed out of the room.

"I don't want anything as big as a house!" I said. "I'm planning to defeat that demon, and I need some money to make my plan work. I believe you said there was ten million eris in it for me if we beat him? Could I ask for an advance—even a little one?"

"Yeah, I remember that. But—and I know I'm the one who brought it up—I think maybe we should call off that deal. I got some more information on the demon… Just recently, one of the most powerful parties in Axel tried to take him down, and they wound up at the Eris church." She sounded worried.

"The Guild only learned about that moments ago, and you've

already heard it. Maybe it's a sign of just how much panic has gripped this town…"

"Oh, no, I was just over there, throwing rocks at the Eris church, and I saw them treating these really badly wounded people, y'know? I bugged them about it and said I wouldn't go away until they told me what happened, and that's how I got the story… Oh! Even for your big sis, that expression of love is painful!"

"Please try to behave yourself, 'Sister'! Don't make this situation any more complicated than it already is!!"

"*Cough…* I wonder if this is what they call hard to get. Well, I can't say I *don't* enjoy it!" Cecily tried to calm me down as I strangled her, finally handing me something.

"Who's playing hard to get, you—? What's this?" The pouch she handed me was noticeably heavy.

"Ten million eris."

"What?!" I looked at the pouch, astonished. "A-are you sure about this?! Just giving it to me? Aren't you worried I might take the money and run?!"

"I *am* a cleric, remember?" Cecily said. "I consider myself an excellent judge of character." A beatific smile spread over her face.

"A-and you aren't worried I might lose this battle? Anyway, what's come over you? You're suddenly so different, I hardly know how to reac—!"

Then she was hugging me. "It's all right. I, Cecily, priestess of the Axis Church, guarantee it. I *know* you can win. My dear, sweet, stalwart Megumin—you wouldn't be defeated by any demon."

"M-miss…"

I didn't know what to do. I felt like I was coming down with a case of the warm fuzzies.

Truthfully, I wasn't altogether confident about fighting that demon.

And at that moment, this woman, usually so flighty and odd, hit me with this sneak attack of kindness...

"Come on—open the bag. And then put it to good use!"

I forced myself to hold back my tears as I opened the heavy pouch in my hand...

...and discovered not money but a large collection of oversize rocks bearing a note that read, *Sucker!*

"Pffft! Oh gosh, Megumin, you should've seen your face—you were almost crying! It was *adorable*! Ahhh-ha-ha-ha, bwa-ha-ha-ha, how can you be so cute?! Joke's on you! That was— Aaaghhh, I'm sorry; your big sister is sorry! I went too far; I apologize! Just please stop pelting me with rocks!!"

3

When I finally got downstairs, I found Yunyun pacing back and forth like a bear in its cave.

"What are you doing, Yunyun? I told you to go kill time somewhere."

"Megumin! Could I just walk away after leaving me with that foreboding speech? I was worried sick about you… Hold on, why does it look like you've been crying?!"

I quickly wiped the corners of my eyes. "N-no reason! No reason at all!"

"You're practically a rock, Megumin, and something made you cry!! What was it?! And did you get our war chest?!" Yunyun had me by the collar, using both her hands, and was shaking violently.

"I have ten million eris right here…"

"What on earth did you do to get ten million eris?!" For some reason, Yunyun was crying now, too, not to mention shouting.

I remembered what Cecily had said earlier:

"Stop, please stop! That was just a little prank because I trust you so much, Megumin! I was so sure you would take care of everything, see?! And I thought I would tease you a little when it was all over… Ahhhh, stop, stop, you don't have to be so mad!!"

"…I don't want to tell you."

"No! Megumin, you've been defiled!"

Yunyun seemed to be under yet another strange misunderstanding, but I couldn't muster the energy to explain; I just trudged out of the inn.

"Listen, Megumin. What's done is done. And we needed that money for a noble cause, to keep that demon from destroying our town. So whatever you did to get it, I won't look down on you or be ashamed of you."

....

"I know this has to be harder on you than it is on me. I mean, it reduced *you* of all people to tears... I can't believe... I just can't imagine... *Sniff...*"

"Oh, will you give it a rest already?! You have the wildest imagination of anyone I've ever met!! I didn't sell my body or something—I just said something a little bit embarrassing to somebody who has a soft spot for me, and then I let them hug me!"

"You said something embarrassing, and then they hugged you?! Was that really all? I mean, as if that weren't bad enough? Was that all it took to make you cry?"

That made me think for a moment. "Well... Afterward, they were unexpectedly kind to me, and I found myself somewhat deceived... Frankly, it doesn't put me in a good light, so I'd rather not share the details."

"I knew it!!"

...Oh, forget it.

"Anyway, I got the money, so what's important is that we use it to wage war effectively. I have somewhere to go, so, Yunyun, you take this to the magical item shop. Buy everything that looks like it might be useful. And do anything else with it that you think will improve our odds in this fight. Oh...and buy a black cat plushie, if you would." I handed her the pouch.

"Huh?! B-but I have no idea what to do with all this money...!"

I would just have to leave the rest to my poor, confused Yunyun.

4

"Please! When we get the bounty, I'll give you all of it!"

"Huh, I don't care if you're going to give us every cent you have; we're talking about *that* demon, right?! It beat the magic-sword guy and Rex and his whole party—we don't stand a chance!"

I was back at the Adventurers Guild, speaking to the adventurers.

"Oh! You there, uh... Well, I forget your name, but we were in a party together once! So you know how strong I am. You'll go demon hunting with me, right?!"

"You could at least remember a person's name! A-and no, I think we'll pass. And that's *because* we've been in a party with you—we don't want to get caught up in your spell..."

"Y-yeah, that's right. And if you miss, we would be completely help-less. That's not a gamble I want to take."

C-crap...

"Oh, you over there! Are you looking for an excellent wizard? I'm from the Crimson Magic Clan! I'm sure I can be of use to you. You need only—"

"No way, no how, I'm not going after any demon! Our whole party is low-level and loving life. An Arch-wizard from the Crimson Magic Clan would completely throw off our balance."

I had decided to swallow my pride and beg everyone who would listen to join me, but my reputation already preceded me, and it wasn't a good one. Between that and the rumors of the demon's strength, no one was willing to take me up on my request.

My plan had consisted of two main things: Yunyun would get some magical items that would help slow the demon down, while I recruited some muscle among the adventurers. If we could catch Host in a trap, maybe we could defeat him before he got his wits about him again—or if not, the adventurers could buy us enough time to get some distance and drop a decisive explosion on his head.

I had been sure it would work somehow, but I had miscalculated.

But then...

"Ummm..."

* * *

I heard a voice behind me, full of hesitation and anxiety.

"You're the one who's always with that Yunyun girl, right? We aren't much, but if we can help…"

I turned around…! "Strength is immaterial if you're willing to help me. I— *You?!* I am looking for adventurers, which neither of you is. This is much too dangerous for civilians. Scram! And stay away from Yunyun!!"

I found myself confronted with the old drunkard and the cruiser, the ones who had been so eager to take advantage of Yunyun at every opportunity. As I was shooing them away, a buzz ran through the Guild.

What could that be about?

As casually as I could, I said to someone nearby, "Say, what's happening?"

"Hrm? Oh, I guess there are these awesome adventurers swearing they're gonna defeat that demon or something. There are only two of 'em, but they went rushing out of the Guild like— Yikes! Wh-what're you doing?!"

I had the guy by the chest. "Who were they?! Describe them to me!"

"O-one of them was, like, a Crusader, I guess? And the other one looked like a Thief… They were both saying stuff like, *'We must defeat the demon!'* and *'We'll kill any demon that wanders through here!'* or something."

If I had gotten here just a moment sooner, I could have recruited them…!

Then again, maybe they would surprise us all and actually defeat the demon.

"But I wasn't able to actually get anyone to help us. This is looking worse and worse…"

5

"How did it go for you? Find any useful-looking items?"

"I went to every magical item shop in town and bought whatever the clerk said were their most powerful items. But..." She presented me with her collection, much of which looked distinctly familiar.

"...These were all made in Crimson Magic Village."

"...Yeah, we're sort of a household name these days."

I wasn't thrilled to be paying top dollar for things we could have procured perfectly cheaply in our own hometown, but knowing their provenance, at least I was confident of their quality.

"Where did you go, Megumin? You must have been doing something to get ready for the battle, right?"

I couldn't quite bring myself to look at Yunyun. "I thought I would find us some allies, but... Let's just say I'm a little too well-known for my own good, and no one was biting..."

"You did this to yourself! Nobody wants to help you, right? Now, what are we going to do? Wizards without front-row protection are sitting Duxions!"

I picked up Chomusuke, who was curling around my feet as if trying to escape the reality of the situation. "Just who do you think I am? Yes, I am the greatest genius of the Crimson Magic Clan and wielder of Explosion! The moment that demon gets anywhere near us, *he* is the one who will be dead! In one hit! ...Oh! Yunyun, look, you've done it! This is a scroll with a spell of concealment within it—with this, victory is ours!"

"I bought it just in case, but I don't know if it will really work, okay? We're facing a high-level demon here; he might be able to see through light-bending magic before we can reach him..."

She trailed off, but it was better than having no plan at all. I tucked the scroll carefully in my bag.

"And here's the black cat plushie you asked for. Not that I have any idea what you want to do with it…"

I took the stuffed toy and silently tied it to Chomusuke.

"Uh…"

"If we leave it like this for a few minutes, this toy will acquire Chomusuke's scent. We simply leave this on some unpopulated part of the plain, hide ourselves with the scroll, wait until that monster takes the bait, and then *bam!*"

"Y-you really think it will be that easy? Come on—it's not too late. We can still run away to some other town…"

…To think that Yunyun, one of the most generous people I knew, had come to be able to say something this cut-and-dried in less than a year. Perhaps this girl really had grown up a bit when I wasn't looking.

Though I wasn't sure I approved of the direction she had grown up *in*.

I showed Yunyun my Chomusuke/plush-toy hybrid.

"It will go well—you will see. You are not the only one who has found themselves attached to this stubborn fluff ball, Yunyun."

Besides…

"Though it was never for long, this town is home to people I have adventured with now. This fur ball and I are the source of this problem. And we will be the end of it!"

I spun on my heel to go back to the inn, but I heard Yunyun behind me, exasperated.

"Gosh. You're just as reckless and stubborn as ever."

I didn't even look back as I said, "Oh, hush. You are just as timid now as *you* ever were, always sticking with the status quo."

I heard Yunyun swallow. And then…

"…But I think I've become a lot more individualistic and matter-of-fact this year."

Did I really hear her say that, or was it just my imagination?

6

Back at the inn, I had my dinner and went back to my room, but then a thought struck me, and I ended up knocking on Cecily's door.

"Are you there?"

"Mm? Megumin, my sweet? Come on in—it's not locked."

I opened the door and found an exhausted Cecily slumped on the bed.

"You look rather tired, don't you? Did you go enjoy yourself somewhere after I left?"

"Don't be sassy. I was so inspired by your dedication, Megumin, that I actually went to work for once—you know how unusual that is?"

Huh!

"And may I ask exactly what sort of work you did?"

"Well, I went to the Eris church..."

"I'm sorry I asked." More fool me.

"Wait, hear me out! Your big sister really worked hard this time! I only know the simplest of healing magic, but I'm very confident in it! And so..."

"No, don't tell me any more. I know what happened: You waited for some poor injured person to drag themselves to the Eris church, then tried to horn in on the church's business?"

"Megumin, you're the worst! I can't believe...! I mean, I would never...... Huh. That's not a bad idea, actually. I'll have to make a note of it."

"Do it later. I came here to talk to you." As Cecily assiduously made a note of my plan, I held out Chomusuke to her, now free from the plush toy. "I need you to look after this cat for a while."

"I can do that—but isn't she sort of your mascot? The one who makes you even more adorable than you are? You really want to leave her with me?"

"The word isn't *mascot*—it's *familiar*. And tomorrow is likely to be witness to a truly brutal battle, so for safety's sake, I'm leaving her with you." Then I put Chomusuke on the bed Cecily was lazing around in. Chomusuke sniffed a few times, perhaps curious about the scent of this stranger, and Cecily patted her on the head.

"Well, then you can count on your big sister. I'll even teach her a trick while she's with me. What would you say to a fire-breathing cat?"

"H-hey, don't teach my cat weird tricks! Well anyway, miss."

"I keep telling you, call me Big Sis Cecily!"

"W-well, C-Cecily, take care of my cat."

Cecily seemed to recognize that this was the best concession she was going to get out of me and appeared satisfied. As I left the room, she was already playing with Chomusuke.

"Huh?! Megumin, what were you doing in there?!" As I left Cecily's room, I ran into Yunyun, who was just heading off somewhere.

"I have an acquaintance in this room," I replied. "For that matter, where are *you* going at this hour?"

Yunyun couldn't quite bring herself to look at me—very suspicious. "W-well, look, I'm an adventurer just like you, and sometimes adventurers go down and check out the tavern at night, right?"

"Yunyun, you've become a ne'er-do-well!"

"No, I haven't! I was just curious, okay?!" she replied hotly.

"…Then I shall accompany you. Poor, gullible Yunyun, you will look as tasty to the patrons of that bar as a whole flock of Duxions would to me if I had been holding in my explosion all day long."

"I-I'll be just fine without you, thank you very much! Come on—I was at the Guild bar all night just recently, and I was fine!"

She really didn't want me to come.

"Okay, see you tomorrow!" she said, and then she rushed off into the night.

7

"…I can't sleep."

My big battle was scheduled for tomorrow. Maybe it was the anxiety that was keeping me awake. Until just a year ago, I had been living a peaceful life as a student in Crimson Magic Village—how in the world was it that I now found myself preparing to fight a high-level demon?

When I thought about it, I realized how full of adventure this past year had really been. The Dark God had been unsealed, and just when I thought its servant had been vanquished, I had to battle Arnes, a powerful demon. And now, in order to protect my new home of Axel, I would have to take on the demon Host. In my entire adventuring life to come, I was sure I would never encounter anything like this again.

Most adventurers took on surprisingly ordinary quests to earn their daily bread. I couldn't find any party unusual enough to accept me, so I didn't know what would become of me even if I did manage to survive the battle with Host…

There in the dark, I buried my head in the blankets. This would never do, letting my thoughts get as dark as the night around me. I was just apprehensive about the next day, that was all.

I lay there, and eventually I had the sense that it was getting brighter outside the window. Somehow, I suddenly found myself wide-awake. I couldn't shake the sense that I was forgetting something important… What could it be? Something very, very important to me— Wait! Ahhh! I had forgotten my daily explosion!

No wonder I couldn't sleep, I thought, and I was just about to get up when:

"*Unlock.*"

I heard a whisper from outside my door and then the *click* of the lock opening. What kind of pervert could be trying to pick the lock to my room at this time of night?

The image of Cecily flashed through my mind as I turned over, back to the door, pretending to be asleep. My fists were clenched so I could attack the intruder at any time.

At length, the door eased open.

"Megumin, are you asleep...?"

I relaxed my fists when I recognized the voice. The intruder was Yunyun. Still, what was she doing sneaking around?

I could have just told her that I was awake—but for some reason, I decided to continue pretending to be asleep.

"...Megumin, you're really something. The way you refuse to run away even in the face of that demon. If I was in your place, I'm sure I'd be awake all night worrying."

I shouldn't have pretended to be asleep. I could hardly get up now that I'd heard her say that...

As I was privately regretting my choices, Yunyun went on whispering, as if to herself. "Honestly? When you decided to learn Explosion, I wondered how the smartest girl in class could be so dumb."

I had a sudden urge to jump out of bed and tackle her.

"And then there was the way you helped that Axis guy in Arcanletia with that ridiculous proselytizing... I mean, come on..."

Yunyun seemed to run out of steam for a moment... Seeing as she was no more innocent than I was in that regard, I thought she should be more careful about bringing it up.

"But..." My back was to Yunyun, so I couldn't see her expression at that moment. "But with Explosion, that one, gimmicky spell, you got rid of the servants of the Dark God; you got rid of Arnes. And now you're going to take on that demon. Megumin..." I couldn't see her face, but I was sure— "Megumin, right at this moment, I think you're the coolest, most incredible person I know."

I had no doubt her face was beet red.

Probably almost as much as mine.

If I was to sit up now, Yunyun would be completely traumatized to realize I'd heard everything she said. But after she had been so honest with me, for once, to be left unable to respond at all...

"I'm sure you already know what's going to happen, Megumin. I'm sure you realize that even if you make yourself invisible with magic, the buildup of MP when you use Explosion will give away your position."

...I could hardly admit at this point that I hadn't thought that far.

I shifted uncomfortably, embarrassed, but Yunyun's tone suddenly changed. "So I... I'm going to borrow this. So that I can keep being your rival, Megumin, awesome as you are."

She sounded so serious. Then I thought I sensed her picking something up. After everything she had said, I didn't need to look to have a pretty good idea what it was.

It must have been the plush toy, the one with Chomusuke's scent on it that I was going to use to draw out Host. She wanted to do it first, to be the one to stop him. But Yunyun didn't have the decisive firepower necessary to do the job. She would never manage it alone.

"I was at the Guild tavern until just a few minutes ago, and I... For the first time, I was finally able to ask someone myself if I could join their party."

......

"It was Rex and his group. You know, one of the top parties in Axel. I said I wanted revenge on that demon, and they took me up on it immediately."

They did?

I thought everyone in that party had been seriously wounded…

"I never was able to find the courage to fight the monster on my own, but with them behind me, I'm sure…"

I listened to Yunyun's confession, trying to decide when I should finally sit up.

"Okay, I'm going now."

It was now or never. If I greeted her sleepily, pretended I had just woken up…

"You're the most important friend I have. I can't let you go to that fight, knowing you can never win. So…" I wanted to respond, but I had no idea how. "Megumin, I'm sorry."

Her apology was so quiet, so gentle.

"*Sleep.*"

I couldn't fight the magically induced fatigue…

8

"—!!"

I leaped out of bed as soon as my eyes snapped open. I looked out the window and beheld a beautiful sunny day. As if to prove that it hadn't been a dream, the cat plushie beside my door was missing.

"She has done it now! For the first time in your life, Yunyun, you have tricked me!!"

First and foremost, I felt bitterness and frustration that she had stolen a march on me. Suddenly, she was the first to join a powerful party, the first to do battle with Host. That might have seemed like all good things, but for me personally…!

"Nothing is more humiliating for a member of the Crimson Magic Clan than having their moment stolen! Do not imagine it will end here!!" I shouted, then grabbed my staff and charged out of the room—

"Eek?!"

"Hrk?!"

—and almost directly into Cecily, who was just outside.

"Sorry! I've got to hurry. This is a bit of an emergency!! See you later!"

"What's going on? Why are you in such a rush? What kind of emergency?"

I didn't exactly have time to regale Cecily with the whole story, but I felt bad leaving her there with no explanation...! I tried to keep a handle on my rampaging emotions as I told her what the situation was. She looked at me curiously. "This adventuring party that went with your friend to slay the demon, Megumin, was it led by a person named Rex?"

"Huh? Yes... You see, I guess they're supposed to be one of the most powerful parties in Axel..."

"I healed them!" Cecily said, giving me a big smile and an even bigger thumbs-up.

"...Huh?"

"I said, I healed them—that party! Didn't I tell you I actually did some work yesterday? I wandered over to the Eris church, hoping to throw a wrench into things somehow, and there they were, moaning and groaning and looking like they were really suffering."

Why did I have a bad feeling about this?

"Well, it looks like my faith in Lady Aqua was greater than the Eris priest's faith in his goddess! He worked on them, but they could still barely move. He just had to stand and watch while I healed them to a point where they could fight, sort of, if they worked really hard at it and really wanted to! Ooh, you should have seen the look on that priest's face!!"

So she was the one who had screwed everything up! Although to be fair, I had never expected Yunyun would consider taking on the battle herself. I'd also assumed that even if someone invited Yunyun to party up with them, no one would be willing to go after that demon—no one except Rex.

And yet, all stupid Cecily had done was heal some injured people, and I could hardly complain about that!

"I can't just stand here—I have to go…!" I was about to rush off again, but Cecily grabbed my arm. "I don't have time to play with you right—"

Then I looked into her face, and the words died on my lips. She was whispering something and looking exceptionally serious.

"The goddess Aqua bestows her gifts upon you! *Blessing!*"

A gentle light shone from Cecily's outstretched hand. It enveloped my body…

"I can barely remember the incantation for anything but that healing magic. I'm so lucky it worked," Cecily said with a relieved smile. I couldn't help but give her a bit of a smile in return. And I couldn't help being a little bit thankful to this strange Axis disciple. With things the way they were, I had started to panic without even realizing it. Thanks to her, I was able to relax a little.

"Miss…"

"I really think you could afford to call me Big Sis by now…"

I smiled again. "Big Sis Cecily… I'm going now."

"Of course. Come back soon!"

9

On the great field outside of town. Even the Giant Toads that normally hopped around the grassy expanse were nowhere to be seen.

"We'll stall him again! You, use the same spell as last time!!"

"G-got it! Leave it to me!"

Instead...

"You think you can stop me? I'd like to see you try! I'm so sick of you small fries!!"

...there were Yunyun and the others, engaged in a sprawling battle with Host, the demon.

"Rex, fall back! You've done all you can!"

"Yeah—your right arm is broken, isn't it?! You're pale as a ghost!"

Host, missing one of his wings from his run-in with the magic-sword wielder, now had cuts and scrapes all over his body. I got the sense that he was weakening.

"Crap... Normally I'd kick your small-fry asses without breaking a sweat, but..."

Terry and Sophie stepped forward to relieve Rex. Host sounded like he was trying to catch his breath.

I observed the goings-on and remarked:

"Now, just look at this. I wonder if it's really okay for me to join this battle..."

The scroll with the light-bending magic had made me invisible, and I was watching from a distance.

Recognizing Host was on the back foot, I was surprised to realize they just might pull this off. I had intended to go charging in, but maybe it would be best if I just watched for a while. This was bad timing for a Crimson Magic Clansperson to make her entrance anyway. It was all well and good to show up at a moment of crisis and save the day, but far be it from me to look like I was just riding the coattails of someone else's victory.

Yunyun brandished her wand in one hand, clutching a little stone in the other. *"Lightning!!"*

I could hear her all the way across the field as she unleashed a bolt of tremendous lightning magic. The same instant the bolt struck, the stone in her hand shattered…!

"Grgh?! Gaaaah, that *hurts!* You and that stupid spell are getting on my nerves! Dammit, I'm low enough on strength that I don't want to use magic if I don't have to, but…!" Host, reeling from the lightning bolt, raised both hands and intoned, "Get lost, twerps! *Inferno!*"

Then he brought down his hands—!

As if knowing what he would do, Yunyun had already dropped her wand and grabbed a scroll with both hands. *"Magic Canceler!"*

The spell that should have come bursting out of Host's down-swept palms fizzled and died. Instead, the scroll Yunyun had pointed at him turned black and crumbled away. The magic within had activated and countered Host's spell.

Yunyun collected the wand lying at her feet and produced another small stone from her pocket. I knew what it was: manatite. It was a mineral that contained magical power, and as an item, it could get dramatically expensive depending on the size and purity of the stone. Yunyun actually seemed to have the upper hand against Host, even if she did need valuable magical items to get and hold it.

"Y'don't give up, do ya, ya little worm? This is why I didn't want to have to tangle with the Crimson Magic Clan!! Fine, you wanna do some target practice? Fire away! Forget bein' clever; I'm just gonna smash you to pieces!"

Now properly upset, Host closed the distance with Yunyun with a speed you wouldn't have expected from a creature of his size. Sophie and Terry moved to cover her.

"We're going with Plan F, everyone!" Yunyun shouted—whatever that meant—and then she took out another scroll and prepared to use it. "I'm ready!"

"All set! Go for it!"

"Come at us!"

This was apparently some tactic they had devised in advance.

"Got another cute idea?! You and your little games—they ain't worked yet…!" Host, unperturbed, charged in…!

At the same moment, Rex and the others covered their eyes. As I watched, wondering what they had in mind:

"*Flash!*" Yunyun exclaimed, followed by a burst of extremely bright light.

"Ha! Us demons don't see things with our eyes! This might be a temp body, but your dumb little trick still won't work on it!!"

"D-damn! …Agh?!"

"Sophie?! Ngah!!"

From the cries, it sounded like Terry and Sophie were down. I heard two *thumps* of something hitting the earth.

"Dammit, it didn't work at all?! I thought for sure I heard a little yelp…!"

I must have judged correctly, because Rex's was the only voice I heard.

Incidentally.

"—! —!!"

The little yelp had probably come from me, where I was still rolling on the ground with my hands over my eyes. They burned with the light, but I worked my way to a crouch, trembling.

"Right, we're down to two of you, then. Any more little plans you want to try?" Host sounded downright triumphant.

I struggled to open my eyes and discovered Yunyun confronting the demon. Rex stood beside her, his massive sword dangling in his left hand. The others were collapsed on the ground, and Terry (I think) looked like he was unconscious.

In response to Host's taunt, Yunyun and Rex quietly conferred.

"Mr. Rex, demons have strong magic defense, so I don't know if this is going to work, but…I do have one item left."

"…All right. What do you need me to do?"

This was troubling. From the vibe, I could tell I could hardly butt in now. Clearly nervous, the voices of the other two finally sank so low that I couldn't hear the last words they exchanged.

"Huh, gonna try again? Cool, give it your best shot! Every time you try one of your dumb tricks, you leave yourselves vulnerable. Next time you fail, one of you two is going down!!" Host mocked them openly, but his golden eyes were clearly suspicious, on the watch.

Then Yunyun pulled out some sort of bottle…

"…? Is that a magic potion?!" As Yunyun went to down the draft, Host charged at her again.

"Leave the rest to me, kiddo!" Rex bellowed and lobbed his sword at Host.

"?!"

Host probably never expected someone to *throw* a weapon at him, and he reacted a second late. He sent the blade flying away with a sweep of his thick-skinned arm. Then the massive limb was thrust in the direction of Rex.

"*Paralyze*!!"

At the exact same instant, Yunyun intoned a spell with all her might after she downed the potion. I was sure that against a demon in a temporary body, paralysis would never—

"Huh! Not very well-informed for a Crimson Magic kid, are ya? Demons aren't affected by p-para— Huh…?!" Host went from triumph to chagrin in an instant.

"Paralyze doesn't work on demons? Believe me, I knew that! I was the second-best student in my class, I'll have you know!"

What Yunyun had just consumed was commonly known as a magic potion. Such a drink could increase the power of a specific spell or kind of magic or, alternatively, it might alter the effects of a spell completely.

From the fact that Host couldn't move, it was obvious the spell had worked. Yunyun hadn't used the potion earlier because it was a gamble on whether it would be effective. A gamble she had won.

Now they just had to finish off the immobilized demon.

"Heh, that's gotta be some potion to bind me, the great and powerful. But I'll bet y'used up a lot of your magic doing that. Think you have enough to finish me off before I'm not paralyzed anymore? With a spell like this, I bet you got a few minutes, tops. You don't get the job done before time's up...and *your* time's up. Y'feel me, little girl?"

The fact that Host had suddenly become a talker again was proof that he was in crisis.

"So I got a proposition for ya. How 'bout we both just go home for today? Don't you want to get some help for your little friends there? I'll make you a promise: If we both call it quits here, then even if this Paralyze wears off immediately, I won't come after you again today. I know y'might not believe me, but a demon never breaks a promise."

Yunyun, apparently unable indeed to believe him, didn't say anything.

Host was starting to get nervous. "...You said you were the second-best student in your class, right? Then you of all people oughta know demons never break contracts or go back on our word!"

Nervous and angry.

"...You've got it wrong," Yunyun said quietly, her voice shaking.

"Wrong? What did I get wrong?" Host asked.

"Ummm... Listen. Your deal, it sounds all right. I mean, the thing about quitting for today." Yunyun's voice was cracking.

And then...

"Hey, wait...a second..."

Rex said from nearby.

"Yeah, don't...worry about us...," Terry said, apparently having come around.

"We'll be just fine," Sophie added, as if to give Yunyun the final push. "So go ahead...finish him off!"

...I, however, understood what had happened to Yunyun.

"Um, well...?" Yunyun still hadn't moved a muscle.

"Hang on. Don't tell me..." Host appeared to have figured it out. "You can't move, either, can ya?"

The whole field seemed to fall silent. At last, Host's uproarious laughter split the air.

"You—you Crimson Magic types! You might be a pain in the neck, but I knew I liked you! Got balls enough to cast Paralyze on *yourself*!!"

As he continued to guffaw, tears streamed down Yunyun's cheeks.

"Look, I don't know how it works! It was the last thing I bought, and it was just marked 'hugely increases Paralyze's power and area of effect'! And all I know is that the pretty shop lady was willing to sell it to me for really cheap!!"

Normally, I would have gotten all over Yunyun for buying something so stupid, but when I saw the empty bottle at her feet, I could only hold my head. A potion that caused spells to affect even the caster? An idea that dumb could have come from only my own father.

"Ahhh, I needed a good laugh. So what's the story, huh? I know you don't exactly trust me, but you got a choice to make. You gonna take my offer or not? I'm stuck like a statue right now; you sure you don't wanna try to finish me off? Hey, you just made today so damn *funny* that I'll say the deal's still on if you want it—how's about that?"

Host sounded mocking again, but he still couldn't move. Rex and the others, who had sounded so sure of themselves a second ago, could only listen in silence.

Perhaps this was the moment.

"Ohhh... A-are you trying to pick a fight?! M-members of the Crimson Magic Clan never back down from a fight! Even if they can't possibly win, they...never...?" Still weeping, Yunyun trailed off.

"Hngh?! Where the hell did you come from?!" Host was just as surprised as Yunyun.

The effects of the scroll had deactivated, and I had appeared out of thin air. Already paralyzed, both my onlookers went stiffer still with shock.

"Hello, everyone. I understand you all can't move."

Quite a thing, for them to go off and leave me like this.

"Don't mind me—I'm just a passing great wizard. You all seem to be having so much fun, now that you've ditched me."

10

"Hey, I know you! You're that spell-caster who was all talk! Great wizard, my ass! What are you even doing here? Get out of the way—it's dangerous!!"

Rex, still unable to get up off the ground—perhaps because of his wounds or perhaps because of Paralyze—sounded downright panicked.

"Megumin…?"

Also immobile, Yunyun sounded hesitant, like a child afraid of being scolded. She looked at me carefully as she spoke.

I didn't respond to either of them. "I forgot to let off my daily explosion yesterday, and then in the middle of the night, just when I was about to get up and do it, *someone* cast sleep magic on me…"

"Grgh?! Y-y-y-you were awake?! Oh no! Don't tell me you were awake for all that?!"

I brandished my staff menacingly in Host's direction. "And now I've been looking for something to do with all this extra magic I've got lying around… Something good to unleash my spell on…"

"H-hey, your—your eyes…! Okay, h-hold on! Let's all just calm down! We can be reasonable about this!" Host said, his voice starting to squeak.

"Megumin, please answer me! How long were you awake?! How much did you hear?!" Yunyun shouted, eyes brimming again.

"How long was I awake? Since about the moment you unlocked my door and whispered, *'Megumin, are you asleep…?'* I suppose."

"Nooooooooooooooooooo! Arrrrrrrrrrrggggghhhhh!" Yunyun cried, her face bright red. She tried to flee, but she was still paralyzed.

"Now, then. You certainly did torment me, oh funny friend of mine who confesses embarrassing things to a person who is actually awake and then paralyzes even herself."

"Aaaaaaah! Stop it—please! Have mercy on me! I'm sorry, I was wrong, just stop! Are you angry that I cast Sleep on you and then went off to fight without you?! That I helped myself to your plush toy?! I apologize for everything—just stop already!!"

"It's very embarrassing, the way you can bring yourself to say,

'*Megumin…you're the coolest, most incredible person I know,*' when no one is listening…"

"Yaaaaahhh! Noooooooooo!"

"'*You're the most important friend I have*'… Yes, when such things are whispered to me, even I cannot simply stand by!!"

"Somebody kill me! I can't run away, I can't move, I can't even end it all myself! Somebody please put me out of my misery!! I can't bear to live anymore! Just kill me now!!"

Yunyun sounded like she was about to break. Host was watching us with something like amusement.

Finally, Rex, who had been quiet until that moment, burst out, "C'mon, Big Mouth! How long are you gonna play around? Just hurry up and………? Wh-what? Hey, what's going on here? You're looking really strange!"

Well, yes.

While I had been busy waging psychological warfare on Yunyun, I had also been gathering my magic.

"The spell I use requires an immense concentration of power. This particular situation is ideal for me."

"You need to concentrate even more? I've lived a long time, kid, but I've never been this freaked out by a magical aura before…" Host was sounding more or less resigned but also a little intrigued.

"I will now unleash my secret technique. It is the same spell that crushed your companion Arnes."

"So you're the one who did her in… I see it now. Magic like this, I don't think she coulda stood up to it."

I felt more magic than usual bubbling up within me, maybe because I hadn't used any of it yesterday. There was so much of it that I could hardly control it all, and the air around me began to vibrate, then crackle with electricity.

"G-geez, what the…? What's going on…? I've been adventuring a whole lotta years, but I've never seen anything like this...," Rex mumbled, finally able to turn his head to look at me. "I can't believe it—you weren't just talk after all...," he said, terrified, his face pale.

I didn't bother responding, just sort of smiled. "Here goes," I said. "My ultimate technique, Explosion!!"

When Host heard the name of the spell I planned to use, he heaved a sigh—a remarkably human gesture.

...I'm not an expert reader of demon emotions, but I think he might be sort of smiling, just like Rex.

"Ah, geez... Y'know, if I were in top shape, I think I could survive that. If I hadn't been attacked by that stupid-tough Crusader and her Thief friend yesterday. Weirdos..."

He was still paralyzed.

"I had this idea, see. I was gonna get 'em back by attacking the town... But all of a sudden, this freaky lady working on building the walls suddenly cast just the *worst* exorcism magic on me..."

It almost sounded like Host was...*complaining.*

"That took out one of my lives. Looks like I'm going to be forced out of my contract with Lady Wolbach... Yeesh, at this rate, I really will end up being summoned by that kid to be her servant."

I didn't really get what he was talking about, but he didn't sound *too* upset.

"*...Explooosion*—!!"

"What the hell is even with this town?! Bozos and weirdos everywhere! Bad news, all of ya! That includes you with your stupid spell! Stupid, stupid—!"

11

Yes, I had destroyed Host, but afterward, with me rendered immobile for lack of magic, Yunyun was the only one out of any of us who could move. The people who came from the Adventurers Guild put us all on stretchers. It was a sorry sight—but that was yesterday. As for right now…

"I knew you could do it! Yes, I always believed in you, my dear, sweet Megumin! Your big sis always knew you would win!!"

Cecily was embracing me warmly in the doorway of our inn; in fact, she was rubbing her cheek vigorously against mine. Which was—I mean, with Yunyun standing beside us and watching, it was sort of embarrassing.

"Um…miss?"

"Call me Big Sis! You did it yesterday!"

"Miss. I'm, uh, getting sort of hot, so if you could let me go…"

"Oh, you're so hot and cold!" She wasn't making sense, but at least Cecily finally released me. She looked me over and, grinning, said, "Are you really sure about this, Megumin? Giving up the entire bounty?"

That's right: I had taken the reward for getting rid of Host and given it all to Rex and his party.

Admittedly, I was the whole reason Host had shown up in this town at all. Or, to be more precise, the reason was the fur ball that was even now curling around my feet.

"Yes, it's fine. I just got the easy part—striking the finishing blow. I wasn't the one who fought a grueling battle against him."

"The way you desperately need money but work so hard to act like it doesn't bother you is just the cutest thing, Megumin!"

"I'm not a-a-acting! It's all true, got it?! I just started to feel like it was sort of my fault that Rex and his party got hurt!"

"Ugh, you can never just come out and say what you're feeling! But I don't dislike that about you!" Cecily was in such high spirits that she seemed about to sweep me up in another hug. I gave her a lopsided smile. "...Okay, then. I hate to say it, but I think it's time for me to go." She hefted her luggage onto her shoulders.

"Will you go straight back to Arcanletia?" I asked.

Cecily grinned like a child with a prank in mind. "Uh-uh, I'm going to go on a journey! I learned something with everything that happened here. Namely, that I can't get by with healing magic alone! I only bothered to learn it in the first place because I play around so much that I tend to get injured. But doing all the stuff I did here, casting Blessing on you and sort of acting like a real priest, it got me thinking. What if I wasn't just a beautiful priestess but a really good one, too? And there you have it!"

Talk about the most shallow reasons.

"Plus, if I reach a certain level, the Church will let me be a branch manager in any town I like!"

Totally shallow.

"...Don't tell me you're angling for a secondment to Axel."

"That's a secret!"

... *That's exactly what she's hoping for.*

"So anyway. Don't get all sad and cry just because I'm not here, okay?"

"I won't... But really, take care of yourself. You really *are* pretty when you keep your mouth shut, so don't get sucked in by some awful man."

"That's supposed to be my line! Listen closely, okay? You need a party, but pick one very carefully!!"

And with that, Cecily left as abruptly as she had arrived...

Yunyun, who had watched the entire exchange silently, was looking very serious.

*   *   *

"Hey, uh, Megumin? Could you come outside of town with me for a moment?"

There beyond the city gates, we found the Giant Toads, previously hidden away in fear of Host, hopping happily around the field. We could see adventurers chasing after them here and there.

"I think this would be a good spot," Yunyun said. She was walking a few steps ahead of me, but she suddenly stopped. And then...

"O my friendly rival, Megumin, called first among the Crimson Magic Clan!" She was blushing crimson but managed to point at me emphatically. "My name is Yunyun! Arch-wizard and wielder of intermediate magic, and she who will one day be chief of our clan! ...I'm going to leave on a journey now. A journey on which I will finally master advanced magic so I can topple you, my rival!"

"...As I recall, it was just the other day that I was not your rival but your most important friend."

"Aaaaah, I can't hear you; I can't hear you!" Yunyun cried, somehow managing to turn even redder.

"Let me guess... Would the real purpose of this journey be to get out of town for a while until the embarrassing things you said blow over?"

"Come on! Even I know better than that! *Ahem*, um. That might... just...be a small part of it... B-but, but anyway!" This time she pulled out her wand and, gripping it tightly, pointed it in my direction. "When I've learned advanced magic, then we'll settle this! ...It kills me to admit it, but you're the one who finished off that demon, Megumin. I finally have to accept that I can't beat you, not as I am now. If I stayed with you here, I would never catch up to you."

"No kidding. As our record currently stands, I believe I am essentially undefeated."

"L-lay off! I'm trying to be serious here; don't throw in your little jabs! Anyway, it doesn't matter! Like I said, once I have mastered advanced magic, then we'll see if you have the nerve to really settle this!" Yunyun was shouting and just about to burst into tears.

I turned so I was facing her directly.

"Very well, so we will. When the time comes, we'll settle this, no tricks—fair and square."

And then I smiled at the rarest of things: a friend.

She Who Will Be Chief of the Crimson Magic Clan!

Two weeks had passed since I'd left Megumin in Axel.

During that time, I had passed through two separate towns, but I still hadn't found any party members... Honestly, I was starting to only half care about finding anyone. The reason being that if you were strong enough, you could level up faster hunting monsters alone. Plus, my goal was to become the greatest wizard of the Crimson Magic Clan. Not to catch up with Megumin but to surpass her. I couldn't shrink from a little danger if that was what I wanted in life. I would probably even have to fight a powerful monster or two. And that meant I couldn't just party up with the first people I saw...!

Or so I kept repeating to myself as I rode along in the tossing, rocking carriage.

What was I going to do? I wanted to cry.

I'm sorry, Lady Eris; it was all a lie and I do want friends, friends I can count on, ideally human ones but who am I kidding? I'll take anything I can have a conversation with at this point. Just give me someone I can adventure with...!

At that moment, someone spoke to me.

"Excuse me, young lady, is something the matter? You keep shaking your head. Are you feeling ill?"

I guess my deep distress had leaked out into my body language. Another woman, older than me, had been kind enough to express concern. I shook a hand in her direction. "No, I-I'm fine—just a little preoccupied! I'm sorry! I didn't mean to act so strangely!" I could feel my face growing hot.

The woman smiled gently at me. "Oh? I gather from the way you look that you're a traveling wizard, but you mustn't overexert yourself, all right?" She handed something to me as she spoke. Baked goods of some kind, neatly wrapped.

"Uh, um…"

"Trust me—these are delicious. Try them for me." She smiled again, and I couldn't object.

"Th-thank you very much…"

Baked goods… Come to think of it, when Megumin and I had been on our way to Axel, we had been in a carriage just like this one, and we had gotten similar treats from an older woman with a child. The memories started to flood over me.

"My goodness, your eyes— are you Crimson Magic Clan?" The woman pulled back her hood and studied me closely. She had unusual golden eyes and short-cropped red hair, and I felt strangely comfortable with her.

"Oh, yes! I'm Crimson Magic Clan and, uh…uhhh… *My name is*—"

She quickly interrupted. "It's all right. You don't have to do the whole song and dance if you don't want to! I know perfectly well how *unique* Crimson Magic Clan names are!"

How very thoughtful of her. For once, I felt like I was meeting someone with a bit of common courtesy.

Evidently, there weren't many travelers today, because it was just the woman and me in the carriage.

"If I may ask," she said as I began to devour the treats, "what is it you've got on your mind? Perhaps I might be able to give you some advice."

"Wh-what have I...? Well, it's a little embarrassing..." I couldn't imagine why I was being so open with someone I had only just met. But nonetheless, I told her about leaving Crimson Magic Village with my friend and going to Axel. I confessed how desperately I had looked for party members and how I still hadn't found any. I told her the whole story of how I had parted ways with one of my oldest friends in hopes of learning enough to become better than her.

The woman listened quietly, then closed her eyes for a moment.

"...Yes, I understand. A long-standing servant of mine happened to depart this world just recently. Good-byes are so painful." She smiled sadly at me. I could tell she had a story of her own.

"Oh, I... I'm sorry to hear that..."

"Oh, no. It's quite all right. This separation is only temporary—it's not as if I'll never see them again, you understand? But back to you... Where is it you're going?"

"Me? Hmm, I guess I hadn't given it much thought, but I want to raise my level as quickly as possible, so I guess I'll find somewhere there are powerful monsters."

The woman nodded knowingly. "Perhaps you'd like to come with me, then? I plan to head to a certain town for a while, for the medicinal waters, mostly—but I wouldn't mind going on an adventure now and again. I may not look like much, but I'm a rather powerf—"

"I'd love to."

I think I startled her, because the woman pulled back ever so slightly. "O-oh, you would? Well... The place I'm going is a city called Arcanletia..."

"Huh?"

I finally got an invitation to go adventuring with someone, and she was going to *Arcanletia*?

The thought of going back to that town, with those people...

"What's the matter? Not too keen on Arcanletia?"

"Urgh... Well, uh... The last time I was there, I might or might not have gotten wrapped up with someone from the Demon King's army."

The words *Demon King's army* made the woman go pale.

"Someone from the Demon King's army...? But plans in Arcanletia weren't supposed to go forward for a long time yet..." She was whispering something to herself, but then she said, "And? What did the Demon King's army do in Arcanletia?"

"Oh, uh. They replaced all the hot-springs water with gelatinous slime."

"Wh-what...?! Are you *sure* it was the Demon King's army? I've n-never known them to come up with such a dumb plan."

"Well, there was a demon lady in town around the same time... So all the Axis followers were saying, '*This has to be the doing of the Demon King. In fact, let's just say* everything *bad that happens in this town is his fault.*'"

"What the heck?!" The woman grabbed me by both arms, but unfortunately, I didn't have an answer for her.

"Anyway, a lot happened, and honestly, I don't really want to go back… You should be careful yourself, okay? There are a lot of strange people there."

"Thank you. Yes, I gathered that from your story."

The carriage dropped its speed and eventually came to a stop.

"It looks like we've arrived at our destination already. I suppose this is where we say good-bye. I have to transfer to a carriage to Arcanletia." The woman let out a disconsolate sigh and got up.

"U-um… I'm really sorry, having to turn you down when you were so kind as to invite me. I've hardly ever been invited by anyone to anything before, so I promise I'll always remember you."

"Y-you don't have to do that! I was just kind of curious about you—you look like you've got powerful magic, and I thought something might come of training you a bit, that's all! You don't have to be so serious about it!" The woman seemed to be panicking a little, but then she turned a gentle smile on me. "All right. Just remember: Getting stronger is important, but making more friends matters just as much, so work hard at both. Otherwise, you'll end up as the Demon King, okay?"

Then she got out of the carriage and waved to me. The carriage slowly started to move again. She watched me go, and I waved at her through the window glass. The last thing she'd said stuck with me:

"Otherwise, you'll end up as the Demon King, okay?"

She was referring to the story of the Demon King. Everyone knew it. The story of the Demon King: strangely named, tremendously powerful, and always alone. The story of the Demon King with his unusual power and his strength, who nonetheless found none of it meant anything all alone—a story we told children to keep them from isolating themselves.

But I was all right. I had that—what could I call her? Companion? Friend? Confidante? …Rival. Yes, I had my rival.

Someday I would surpass her and become the chief of the Crimson Magic Clan…!

That was the promise I made myself as I watched the woman grow smaller in the distance. And then I realized something:

"I forgot to ask her name!"

Epilogue

My name is Megumin.

Greatest genius of the Crimson Magic Clan and wielder of Explosion.

Also, destroyer of the servants of the Dark God and vanquisher of two high-level demons.

"We have room for three more frontline fighters here!"

"Any Priests around? We've got a nice, easy goblin hunt! We need one more person!"

And here I was…

"S-sooo hungry…"

…starving practically to death.

It was another day at the Adventurers Guild. Another day of making a flyer looking for a new party and then sitting in the corner.

How had it come to this?

I had given the bounty I'd earned to Rex and his party, but surely the other adventurers were at least aware that I had defeated Host. So why wouldn't anyone bring me into their fold? When Yunyun left on her journey, I'd given her the remainder of our "war chest" for fighting Host as a going-away present in a foolhardy attempt to look cool.

No, that wasn't true. It was because I had been so certain that I, slayer of the demon, would soon be buried in invitations to join every party around. Money, I had assumed, would not be a problem.

And yet, here we were.

"Yo, whatcha doing here? Still no party?"

I heard someone over my head where I was slumped on the table. I didn't have to look up to know who it was. Rex.

"What is this? Are your injuries healed already? And you felt the most important thing to do after that was to come and mock me? Have you sought me out for a fight? My stomach is empty, meaning my temper is volatile, and I will be more than happy to accept any fight you wish to pick. Crimson Magic Clan members never back down."

"N-no, that's not why I'm here! Why would I ever pick a fight with you? G-geez, lay off—I didn't mean it that way!" I hadn't even looked up from the table, but I had Rex pretty shaken up. "…Hey, this is just a thought. But if you don't have a group to join, why not be part of my party?" He was trying to sound casual, like he was asking me out to dinner…

My head snapped up, and I grabbed Rex's belt. "What did you just say?!"

"Yikes! I just asked if you wanted to join my party. We're making quite a name for ourselves around here. I think we could find a place for you and your awesome magic, y'feel me?"

An invitation to an elite party—for me!

"Details! Give me details!"

"Y-yeah, sure. It's like, you know. None of the monsters around here are worthwhile opponents for us anymore. So, like…" Rex jerked his thumb at the doorway. Sophie and Terry were standing there, looking like they were ready for a very long trip.

......

"We're gonna pick up and go to the capital—you know, the front lines—and make ourselves some real money."

I had to admit, it was a very attractive proposition.

"There should be powerful enemies there, and lots of 'em. Even with just one shot a day, I think you could make a big difference."

It might be a boon to my future if I went with Rex and his party. But...

"The capital. I think that's a lot to ask of someone as low-level as I am," I said, releasing Rex's belt.

"Huh?! Whatever, kid—if it gets to be too much, we'll be there to back you—"

"And another thing," I interrupted. "I've only been in this town for a short while, but I've grown quite fond of it." Then I smiled at him.

"...You're a strange one. Well, I guess that puts you in good company around here, eh?" He grinned. "All right. We're heading out, then. Sounds like some general of the Demon King's is on the move. No time like the present if we're gonna hit the capital and make our mark."

He turned, waving over his shoulder without looking back as he walked over to his companions. I watched him go, feeling overcome with an emotion I couldn't describe, when I realized something:

Crap! This isn't the time to be acting all cool!

I should have at least asked him to treat me to a meal before he left...!

Well, too late for that now. I headed for the bulletin board to check the posts. All the same parties as usual, I assumed.

Argh, so hungry.

I couldn't afford to be choosy any longer. I would take any party I could get—if they wouldn't let me join them, maybe I could at least get a meal out of them.

And that's when I saw a flyer that had never been there before.

They were looking, it alleged, only for advanced classes. A rather high bar in this town of beginner adventurers, but I just happened to clear it. I was disturbed, though, by the postscript: **Current party members: one novice Adventurer, one exceedingly talented and beautiful Arch-priest.**

I was starting to become something of a connoisseur of these bad feelings. The way this person described her own self as a brilliant, beautiful Arch-priest made me think of a certain person who had left town just the other day.

But again, beggars couldn't be choosers. What party could this be...?

When I saw the pair I was looking for, I froze. It was those two people, the ones I seemed to keep running into. It didn't look like anyone had come to talk to them. Maybe the tenor of their post had something to do with it.

"...Maybe we need to lower our standards a little. I get that we're trying to defeat the Demon King here, but the part that says, 'Only those of advanced classes need apply' is probably putting people off," the boy said.

The girl, the one with blue hair, was slumped across the table, looking eminently bored. "Uhhh... But... But..." She didn't want to bend. I assumed she was the one who had written the post. That would make her the (self-professed) beautiful Arch-priest, then.

...*Arch-priest.*

A beautiful Arch-priest with blue hair?! Without meaning to, I almost started to giggle. No wonder no one had found her despite a town-wide manhunt. It was a rude thought, but I couldn't help thinking it as I watched her lie dejectedly on the table.

Still, I couldn't help thinking that joining up with these two seemed likely to make life difficult—even if maybe I wasn't one to talk.

"At this rate, no one's going to show up," the guy said. "Anyway, you might be an advanced class, but I have the lowest job there is. How can I hold my head up if my entire party's full of elite characters? Let's cast a wider net, please...?"

Despite my apprehension, I approached the table where they sat and, endeavoring to sound every bit the cool, collected wizard, said, "I saw the notice seeking adventurers of advanced classes. Is this the right place?"

I ignored the bad feeling. These two... Every time I saw them around town, they seemed to be having fun. I was a "strange one," evidently, and I thought things might not be all bad with them.

This was Axel, the town for novice adventurers.

I had thought I would simply be passing through, but it was starting to look like I would be here longer than I'd expected.

The two of them looked at me blankly. I gave a great flourish of my cape and declared—!!

"My name is Megumin! Arch-wizard and wielder of the most powerful of all offensive magic, Explosion!"

Author/Natsume Akatsuki

Hello, it's Natsume Akatsuki, your author who can also smash beer bottles like boards with a bare hand. The *An Explosion on This Wonderful World!* spin-off series is finally complete! There's no end to the people who helped me finish these books, including Kurone Mishima-sensei, my editor and the entire editorial staff, the designers and proofreaders, the salespeople, and on and on, including, most of all, my precious readers who have made it this far. As an expression of my profound thanks, I'd like to present a beer-bottle break right here and now, but I don't have enough pages for it—real shame.

Welp, I hope to see you over in the main *Konosuba* series! Thank you so much for buying, and reading, this book!

Illustrations/Kurone Mishima

Kurone Mishima here. What a pleasure it's been to handle the illustrations for the spin-off! May all Crimson Magickers live happily ever after!

Design

Yuuko Mukadeya (Mushikago Graphics)
Nanafushi Nakamura (Mushikago Graphics)

Editing

Kadokawa Sneaker Bunko Editorial Section

🔥 CAST 🔥

Megumin	Yunyun	Chomusuke

Cecily

Lain Sheyka

Lin	Keith	Taylor

Jack · Thomas · Rod

Lex · Terry · Sophie

Kyouya Mitsurugi

Host

Aqua · Kazuma Satou

🔥 **SPECIAL THANKS** 🔥

Darkness
Everyone in Axel
All the Axis Believers
All the Eris Believers

An Explosion on This
Wonderful World! 3
The Strongest Duo's Turn

—FIN—

"KONOSUBA!"

GOD'S BLESSING ON THIS WONDERFUL WORLD!

WATCH SEASON 1, 2 & OVA

WATCH ON 🅒 crunchyroll™